THE DETENTION DETECTIVES

LIS JARDINE

PUFFIN

PUFFIN BOOKS

UK | USA | Canada | Ireland | Australia
India | New Zealand | South Africa

Puffin Books is part of the Penguin Random House group of companies
whose addresses can be found at global.penguinrandomhouse.com.

www.penguin.co.uk
www.puffin.co.uk
www.ladybird.co.uk

First published 2023

001

Text copyright © Lis Jardine, 2023
Illustrations copyright © Glenn Thomas, 2023

The moral right of the author and illustrator has been asserted

Set in 12/18pt Sabon LT Std
Typeset by Jouve (UK), Milton Keynes
Printed and bound in Great Britain by Clays Ltd, Elcograf S.p.A.

The authorized representative in the EEA is Penguin Random House Ireland,
Morrison Chambers, 32 Nassau Street, Dublin D02 YH68

A CIP catalogue record for this book is available from the British Library

ISBN: 978-0-241-52338-4

All correspondence to:
Puffin Books
Penguin Random House Children's
One Embassy Gardens, 8 Viaduct Gardens, London SW11 7BW

For Mum, Dad and Grannie Mollie,
with thanks for all the stories.

CASE 1:
Mr Baynton's Murder

WHO'S WHO

Kids:

Jonathan (Jonno) Archer	Me, aka the new kid at Hanbridge High School
Daniel Horsefell	*Star Trek*-obsessed brainiac
Lydia Strong	Nosy and unstoppable 'journalist' from my class
Tyler Jenkins	School bully
Jerome Herrera	Tyler's mate, also unpleasant

Max Archer — My sometimes cute, sometimes annoying little brother

Teachers of Hanbridge High:

Mr Baynton	PE teacher, deceased
Mr Scouter	Headteacher
Mr Packington	Maths teacher
Mrs Sudely	English teacher
Mr Frantock	Deputy Head, science teacher
Miss Black-Dudley	Science teacher
Ms Zheng	PE teacher
Mr Chayning	Psychology teacher
Mr Peters	RE teacher
Miss Culham	School librarian

Other adults:

DI Meek	Police detective in charge
DS Norman	Police officer assisting in murder enquiry

Mrs Fustemann	School secretary, aka The Dragon
Zaara Hussam	Apprentice office administrator
Mrs Scouter	Accountant to the school and wife of Mr Scouter
Anneka Archer	My zany Swiss mum
Iain Archer	My undertaker dad
Lois Baynton	Yoga instructor, and Mr Baynton's wife
Becky Horsefell	Daniel's mum
Gran Strong	Lydia's gran
Stan Waldron	Local entrepreneur and bodybuilder
Valda Campbell	Bristol Town Hockey Club administrator

Please note

Just because I'm the one writing this down, don't go thinking I'm some kind of sidekick. I'm nobody's Dr Watson.[1] I'm as much a detective as either of the others, probably even more so.

But *one* of us had to record what happened. It's a kind of insurance policy, see? A way to tell the world (and the police) what we suspect. And who's probably behind it, just in case something happens to us . . .

Signed,
Jonno Archer
The Detention Detectives

1 Lydia is making me explain my references, because apparently not everyone knows murder mysteries and *Star Trek* as well as me and Daniel. So: Dr Watson is the housemate of the great detective Sherlock Holmes and the narrator of the Holmes stories. If you didn't already know this, you should definitely be watching more TV.

1

Tuesday 13 May, 9.15 a.m.

Hanbridge High School playing field

I knew Mr Baynton was dead as soon as Daniel opened the trunk in the sports equipment shed. We were only in there looking for a football to play with while we waited for the PE teacher.

And there he was.

Dead.

Kids aren't supposed to find bodies. Bodies are just for Sunday evening murder-mystery TV shows, and bedtime reading (as long as Mum doesn't catch me nicking one of Dad's blood-and-guts thrillers).

So all in all, my second week at Hanbridge High was a memorable one. Just not in a good way. But

I'm getting ahead of myself. Let me explain how I got in this mess in the first place.

When Mum dropped the bombshell, that Sunday in January, I'd been sitting at the kitchen table surrounded by my homework and moaning about my DT project getting squashed on the Grensham school bus.

'Well, Jonathan,' she'd said. 'You won't much longer have to put up with all this inconvenience.' Mum's native language is Swiss German, so she sometimes says things in English in a confusing order (she speaks Italian, Spanish and Hungarian too, meaning she can tell me off in *many* different ways). 'Soon you'll be beginning a new school, because we're moving to Nanna Rosie's old house in Hanbridge.'

Well, obviously I didn't believe her. Not until she laid it all out.

'Last week your father applied for a promotion at the Bristol branch of the undertaker's.' (Yes, my Dad's a mortician. Yes, it's a bit weird, but I also think it's kind of cool.) 'And if he gets it, then you will start at a new school in May, and we will be moving finally into our own home!' She leaned over the table and touched my hand. 'You always loved staying in Nanna Rosie's old house. You and Maximilian will finally have a garden to play in, and you shall feel like you are on holiday all the time! Nanna and you would always be talking about her murder-mystery books – they will all be there too.'

I thumped my hands down on the table, either side of my half-eaten cinnamon roll. 'That's ridiculous! Cos Nanna's not around any more, is she? I've only been in Year Seven at Grensham for a term, and *all* my friends are here, the basketball team, the band . . . moving is just not an option, Mum. No way.'

Mum folded her arms in that terrifying way that she does. 'Jonathan. You must try and think about someone other than yourself for one minute! Nanna wanted us to inherit her house. There'll be no rent to pay, and no horrible landlord like Mr Franklin making all of the decisions. We are very, very grateful to Nanna for her kindness to us.'

'Holy . . . crud, Mum. You actually mean it.'

Mum covered Max's ears as he sat squidging Play-Doh on his highchair. '*Tsk, tsk, tsk.* You must not say these words, Jonathan! You must think about the impression you will be making at your new school. No one will want to be friends with such a potty-mouth.'

I spent the rest of the day in a daze. I kept thinking, *When Dad gets back from work, he'll see sense and blow the whole plan apart.* But when he got home, he was all flushed. He picked Mum up and swung her around and kissed her like I wasn't even looking.

'I got it!' he shouted, and they both did a weird jumpy dance around the kitchen.

'So what?' I said.

Mum looked at Dad and shrugged. 'He is not so happy with this plan as we hoped.' She squeezed my cheek. 'Can you not see that your father is pleased to be going back home where he grew up, Jonathan? You are spoiling the excitement of all of us.'

That was the point. And as far as I was concerned, their excitement could stay spoiled.

Mum and Dad might move us to Hanbridge, but there was no way we were going to stay there long.

Looking down at Mr Baynton in that big plastic box felt like the next disaster in a recent string of catastrophes in my life. I grabbed the lid off Daniel and shut the trunk again, quick.

I turned away but I could still see the image when I shut my eyes. Sometimes I wish I didn't notice everything all the time.

Daniel gagged and staggered out of the shed to be sick in the hedge, just missing Tyler Jenkins's Adidas trainers. Tyler was not pleased.

'Oi! W-what do you think you're doing? You'll be a deader if you've got even *one* spot of spew on my new shoes!'

Lydia Strong came running when she heard Tyler's howl of fury.

'Why's Daniel puking? What's in the shed?'

The other students smelled trouble, literally. They started crowding round Daniel, making me feel a bit small and lonely.

I decided to make myself useful by standing in front of the shed door, to preserve the crime scene until the police turned up. I'd read enough murder mysteries and seen enough crime dramas to know how important it was to protect the evidence. I was sweating and feeling a bit sick myself, but it helped ease the quease to concentrate on keeping the rest of the class out of the way. And most importantly to consider the facts of the case: why, what, where, when and who.

Tyler turned away from the crowd and got right up into my face.

'C'mon, new boy, t-tell us what's going on,' he growled. At the sniff of a potential fight, the others left Daniel's side and jostled towards me.

Tyler Jenkins was trouble. I knew that after only one week at Hanbridge High. He was scarily huge for a Year Seven, with an Adam's apple and razor burn – he made the rest of us look like toddlers. And no one ever mentioned his stammer. I suspected the last person who'd made fun of Tyler had ended upside down in a dumpster. I groaned inside, but I stayed where I was and tried to look like I knew what I was doing.

Meanwhile Lydia, stuck behind the group, had started jumping up and down to try and see through the window instead. It didn't work.

'Daniel only chucks up at icky stuff, so there's got to be a reason,' she called over. 'Come on. Spill the tea.'

She squirmed her way through the pack and leaned hopefully against the open door right next to me. Tyler loomed, Lydia stared, everyone else shoved.

I didn't cave in. You don't see Inspector Morse[2] giving a tour of the crime scene to passers-by. I gave the lot of them my best scowl, and kept the door blocked when Lydia tried her best to slip past me.

'Someone go and tell a teacher – get them to ring nine-nine-nine!' I shouted over the noise.

No one moved.

Daniel finally stopped spewing and stood on the edge of the crowd, looking at me all wide-eyed, pasty and confused. He wasn't my idea of back-up, but he'd have to do.

'Daniel! Call the police!' I yelled again, over the horde. He nodded weakly and set off shakily towards the office.

It took ages for anyone to come.

I was barely holding out against the crush when Mr Scouter, the headteacher, finally came puffing across the field, red-faced and breathless.

'Get away from there!' he roared at the mob. 'Yes, you lot! What on earth do you think you're playing at?'

---

2 Inspector Morse is a TV legend, a fictional god of detection. He's Detective Chief Inspector for the Oxford police and solves stuff practically in his sleep, with his trusty assistant Lewis. Nanna Rosie used to record every episode because she *definitely* had a crush on him.

As they backed off, he marched up to me and grasped me by the shoulder.

'Good grief, boy, are you all right?' His face was round and worried, with the size of moustache I've only ever seen on *Magnum PI*.[3] 'Go and sit down over there until the police arrive; they might want to question you.' He turned round. 'The rest of you, get to the hall and wait for Mr Frantock. He'll give you some work to do until next period.'

The rest of the class groaned and moped off, Lydia and Tyler shooting me looks as they passed. I could tell Mr Scouter wanted to look at the crime scene without me there, so I walked a few metres away from the shed and flopped down on to the ground, steering well clear of Daniel's sick spot.

For the millionth time I wished I was back in Grensham with my old mates – Jayden, Kinsey and the rest of the gang – having a *normal* sort of morning. All we did was hang out and play basketball and practise epic rock riffs on our guitars, but it was great fun. Our band, The Boomerangs, was really starting to get noticed.

---

3 Nanna Rosie fancied Magnum too. He was brilliant, a mega-glam 1980s American TV detective, who solved crimes in Hawaii.

They'd probably be looking for a new lead guitarist by now.

As I carried on sitting there, I started thinking about poor Mr Baynton, and what could have happened for him to end up like that. After a few minutes Daniel came back from the school office, and Mr Scouter made him sit down next to me. I glanced at him out of the corner of my eye. His eyelids were pink and he was lightly quivering. I kept my face steady, ready to answer any questions.

I didn't really know Daniel, or anyone else around here for that matter. He was in a couple of my classes; a bit of a brain but not Mr Perfect. He was late for tutor group sometimes in the mornings, and I'd seen him get told off for looking at his phone in the corridors. I was glad Tyler had already gone in. He saw solitary types like Daniel as easy meat, and I didn't want to be labelled as prey by association.

The police finally arrived, along with an ambulance and a white van with 'Forensic Services' on the side. A tall, plain-clothed policeman cornered Mr Scouter at once.

'You're the headteacher? I'm DS Norman, Avon and Somerset Police. Do you mind answering a few questions?' As he flipped open his notepad, I casually leaned forward from my seated position, pretending to pick at the grass, so I could listen in.[4]

'Can you confirm the identity of the deceased, Sir?'

'Oh, yes. It's Ollie Baynton, one of our PE teachers.' Mr Scouter paused solemnly. 'A horrible shock.'

'I see. And what time was the school locked up last night?'

'Hmm. The governors' meeting yesterday evening lasted until around eight thirty. There were a couple of stragglers – the vicar wanted a somewhat premature chat about Harvest Festival – but I made sure everyone was off the premises by around nine p.m.' Mr Scouter rubbed his moustache, leaving it all rumpled.

I wondered if I should be taking notes. Columbo[5] definitely would.

'So would Mr Baynton have been in school until then?'

---

4 Don't judge me, you'd have listened too. Anyone who likes to solve a good mystery would.

5 Another of Nanna's favourite TV detectives from the 70s. Famous for his cigar and pulled-through-a-hedge-backwards appearance. Solved crimes by basically pestering suspects until they confessed. Mum seems to like using this technique on me.

'Let's check you over, boys,' one of the medics said, blocking my view of this interesting conversation. Mr Scouter and the police officer moved into the shed, and out of earshot. The medic took our blood pressure and made Daniel put his head between his knees for a bit, wrapping him in a crinkly silver blanket.

Daniel and I sat quietly for ages. I didn't wonder at the time what he was thinking about, but as it turned out he had plenty to mull over.

2

Tuesday 13 May, 10.20 a.m.

Hanbridge High School playing field

A loud noise broke our quiet when an old Volvo drove across the school field. A middle-aged man got out and started to pull on a white paper onesie. Then he lifted a heavy leather holdall out of the car.

'In the shed, is it?' he asked us cheerfully. His hair was curly and brown and he strolled over to us like he was out for a jolly walk in the country.

'Yeah – the police are in there already,' I said.

'Dr Jeffery Hinton, County Pathologist.' He shook my hand; his was warm and very strong. 'Here to determine cause of death. I deduce by your presence that you are involved?'

'Me and Daniel – we found him.'

'Ah, and Daniel. Pleased to meet you.' Dr Hinton reached out and shook the silent Daniel by the hand too. 'Well, I'd better examine your corpse! See what I make of outward appearances.' The doctor tramped off into the shed, hailing his police colleagues merrily.

Dr Hinton came out again after a few minutes and lit up a cigarette. 'Apologies. Filthy habit,' he remarked as he saw me looking. 'You found the deceased? Bad business. You don't look too shocked, though. Objectionable chap, was he?'

'What d'you mean?'

'I mean was he an unpleasant piece of work? A lot of my PE teachers were.'

I tried to remember what Mr Baynton was like. I'd only had one of his lessons so far.

'Well – he was OK. He looked as if he liked to show off a bit.'

Daniel spoke up for the first time. 'He *does* like to show off. He's all shiny black designer joggers and expensive trainers. And he has this personalized silver whistle that he wears on a chain round his neck.'

My insides twisted. *Don't think about his neck.*

13

But as soon as Daniel spoke, I realized what had been missing.

'I see. And did you notice anything else, observant children?'

I knew he was teasing us, trying to make us squirm. Perhaps *you* shouldn't read the next bit, actually, if you've got a weak stomach.

Because I had noticed a thing or two. Nanna's detective novels were usually pretty tame, but when your dad's a mortician you tend to find a lot of interesting textbooks left lying around the house to do with dead bodies. Not to mention the mortuary supplies catalogues. Mum had been horrified when she'd found a couple of the more gruesome ones hidden under my bed for light reading. Dad called it my 'morbid curiosity'.

'He was strangled,' I said, remembering the bruised marks round Mr Baynton's neck.

'Aha! An expert. How very precocious.' Dr Hinton's grin was smug. 'But did you see his hand?' The pathologist held out his own in a tight fist.

'No . . .' I shook my head. As much as I enjoyed reading Dad's catalogues, in real life I hadn't seen a real body, not before that first glimpse of Mr Baynton's.

'Classic cadaveric spasm! Clutching a bit of paper, I think. Not seen such a nice example of that in ages. I look forward to breaking the proximal interphalangeal joints later to get it out.'

Dr Hinton's laughter made my stomach churn like I was riding the Big One at Blackpool. Daniel got up and stomped off down the field. He didn't come back again until Dr Hinton had gone.

Little did we know, then, that we would get more and more mixed up in Mr Baynton's case.

This was just the beginning.

3

Tuesday 13 May, 10.45 a.m.

Hanbridge High School playing field

The police and the scene-of-crime people were poking around inside the shed for ages while we just sat there, missing our food technology class. Daniel and I didn't speak. I was desperate to get my phone out and message the old gang, tell them what was going down, but Mr Scouter was keeping an eye on us while he talked to the police officer again.

'As I said, Detective, I would have expected Mr Baynton to be on his way home no later than about six. We don't expect our teachers to work excessive hours here at Hanbridge High,' Mr Scouter explained.

16

'And he definitely couldn't have gained access to the school after it was locked up?' DS Norman asked.

'Not with just a teacher's pass. Myself and the *senior* staff, plus a couple of reputable local-community members who run evening classes here, all have authorization, but the majority of the regular staff – no. They'd set the alarms off if they tried.'

'Very well, sir. That's all for now, but we might need to follow up on some of this again later.'

DS Norman came over to talk to us next.

'Hello, lads,' he said. He crouched down so he didn't loom over us, with his leather notepad open and a pen in his huge hand.

I looked around. Weren't they going to ask an adult to supervise while they interrogated us? Maybe there were enough other officers nearby to make it OK.

An older-looking police officer came and stood next to the DS, planting her feet sturdily on the grass and clasping her hands behind her. 'Yes, hello to you both. I'm Detective Inspector Meek, and this is my sergeant, DS Norman. Mr Scouter tells me that you protected the crime scene for us, Jonathan.

Thank you very much for that. Just wanted to ask if you spotted anything in the shed or outside it before you found the body? I mean, ahem, Mr Baynton. Did you pick up any litter, or paper or anything?'

I shook my head, still trying not to think too hard about it. But I clocked the question, just the same.

'No,' Daniel said. 'We weren't really noticing anything, and then we noticed too much.' He took a shaky breath.

'OK. Is the shed normally open, do you know?'

Daniel looked over at me and I shrugged. I'd only been there two weeks; how would I know?

'I think it's normally locked until the teacher gets here. It was open when we found . . . him,' he said.

The police didn't have anything else to ask. They gave us each a card with the Crimestoppers number on it, in case we remembered anything, and told us to take it easy.

After they'd gone, Daniel touched my arm.

'They'll be shutting school for the rest of today, I expect. Do you think one of your parents would give me a lift home?' He looked at me with big Labrador eyes.

'I doubt if mine will be able to come and get me.' I shrugged. 'Mum's at the office all day, and it's her first week so I don't think she'll be able to get away.'

I didn't mention Dad, who'd be at the funeral director's. I couldn't see him asking for time off from a brand-new job either, but especially not just because his son had seen a dead person. Dad's well used to seeing bodies. He collects corpses from the hospital mortuaries all the time. They use this fake trolley that looks like a freshly made bed, and the body is hidden in a secret compartment under the sheets so it doesn't freak out all the hospital patients. And the van is labelled 'Private Ambulance' instead of 'Death Wagon', for obvious reasons.

But I kept those details to myself, because for some reason people get weird when I tell them about this sort of stuff.

Not knowing what to do next, we trudged over to the school office.

Mrs Fustemann, the school secretary, was busy answering the phones in reception. She seemed flustered; perhaps they hadn't had much practice with stuff like this? I suppose it's not every day you find a dead body on school grounds, though she didn't look like the type to offer up a hot, sweet cuppa and a supportive hug, anyway.

She was on the phone when we walked in, her long shiny nails tapping anxiously on the desk.

It turned out she was talking about me.

'*No*, Mr Archer, Jonathan is not able to stay here today. The whole school is closed to students and your son will need to find somewhere else to go if neither you nor your wife are able to leave work. Yes, I *know* he needs to be supervised.' She glanced up at us with flinty eyes. 'Would you be willing to let him go to another pupil's house for the day? He has just come in with a classmate, Daniel Horsefell.'

She put her hand over the phone. 'Daniel, would it be OK if Jonathan came home with you today?'

Daniel looked at me, unsure.

'My mum ... she's a little poorly at the moment ...' he muttered.

'Mr Archer? I've arranged for Jonathan to go to his friend Daniel's house for the rest of the day. Yes, I'll get him to text you with an address. That's all right, Mr Archer. Goodbye.'

Trust Dad to abandon me to the care of total strangers.

'Right! That's settled. But before you go, Mr Scouter would like to talk to you both,' Mrs Fustemann said after she put down the receiver. 'Go through into the office and wait – he's at an emergency meeting in the staffroom at the moment, but that should be over soon.'

Mrs Fustemann buzzed the door open for us as we passed through reception and into the school foyer.

I moved to the right to wait outside the headmaster's office door, but Daniel had the opposite instinct, so we nearly body-slammed into each other.

'Where are you going?' I asked.

'*Shhh!*' he hissed, beckoning me over to the closed staffroom door, as the noise of an intense conversation drifted into the corridor.

4

Tuesday 13 May, 10.55 a.m.

Hanbridge High School office

'Did you hear that?' Daniel whispered, all big-eyed and alert like a puppy who'd heard the word 'walkies'.

'Did I hear what?' I hadn't been paying much attention, my mind on my dad not bothering to come get me, but Daniel's tone made me want to put my ear to the door too. As it happened, I'd been doing quite a bit of eavesdropping at home over the past few weeks, unwilling to let Mum and Dad spring any further surprises on me.

Daniel put his ear to the keyhole to hear better. I looked all around; there was no one about to pay any attention to what we were doing. All the other pupils

22

had left by now, and all the teachers were together in the staffroom, discussing the morning's events.

'Yes, she's the obvious suspect, I suppose. But could she have done it?' A man was speaking over the top of the other voices. 'I thought she was turned away by Mrs Fust–'

'I reckon it was a cult!' interrupted a very high-pitched voice, talking fast and frightened. 'You read about all sorts these days in the papers! I bet they got over the fence to perform their mind-altering rituals and murdered Mr Baynton, or something!'

I concentrated harder, interested to hear what their theories were. It felt personal, having been one of the first to see the body, and I had a certain interest in crime and investigation, after all. My fascination with detectives and death had even got me a nickname back at Grensham – particularly when my pals also realized my dad was an undertaker. Nothing cool, like Campion[6] (who was my favourite detective) or, I dunno, Sherlock. They'd called me 'Morticia' ever since Jayden saw *Addams*

---

6 Albert Campion is another sleuth, this time from the 1930s. He's really posh and funny, but hard as nails, and he's friends with loads of dodgy characters who help him solve crimes, when they're not committing their own. It'd be like recruiting Tyler to help bring down the rest of the school bullies.

Family Values and reckoned I had the same look, especially that time I put on black eyeliner for a Boomerangs rehearsal.

The volume of conversation from inside the staffroom was getting louder.

'To be honest, I can think of a few of us who would have liked to see the back of him,' I heard Mr Packington say. 'He was a nasty little man, always making jokes about my hairline, and leaving shampoo suggestions in my pigeonhole.' Mr Packington was my maths teacher, and from my minimal encounters with him had seemed pretty laid-back, but I could tell from his sharp tone that Mr Baynton had been getting on his nerves.

'Too right!' came a woman's voice from the far side of the room, muffled by distance. 'Stole my milk out of the fridge more than once, then swaggered around drinking it right in front of my eyes! No one ever pulled him up on it.'

'He certainly was, er, something of an *acquired* taste as a colleague,' Mr Scouter said. 'However, we mustn't speak ill of the dead. As the leaders of this school, it falls to us to set a sensible example for our students.' Mr Scouter's words cut through the general babble and the staff went quiet. 'Our role here is to reassure them at this time. If we all go throwing around foolish suggestions as to why Mr Baynton met his end, the gossip and wild theories will multiply, and before long they'll all be having hysterics in the hall, thinking Ms Zheng is coming to get *them* next.'

The teachers all tittered awkwardly – this was obviously an in-joke we had missed. I heard an angry *hmm* – probably from Ms Zheng, disapproving of such silliness at her expense.

Once they'd quietened back down, Mr Scouter spoke again.

'The police will spend this afternoon asking each of you your whereabouts since the end of school yesterday. I have no doubt you will all do your best to be helpful and professional, but I suggest that no one leave the grounds until those interviews have been concluded. And they will certainly need to look at all paperwork connected with Mr Baynton. Again, I imagine this won't be an issue, because I am certain you will have dotted every *i* and crossed every *t*, with regard to the administration of your departments.'[7]

---

7 Mr Scouter speaks like a textbook a lot of the time, which isn't a problem for me, but is for the thick-headed – e.g. Tyler Jenkins.

At this last comment, the murmuring started up again.

I looked out of the corner of my eye. Daniel had relaxed a bit now. I wondered what he'd overheard that had first grabbed his attention and made him so nervous?

'DI Meek assures me that they will allow us to reopen the school to pupils tomorrow, although the crime scene may be taped off for some time yet, of course. No doubt Ms Zheng is already working out where to find alternative sports equipment for the scheduled lessons.'

'Of course, headmaster. In fact, I should get over to the PE office now to make sure, as you suggest, everything is tidy for the police,' Ms Zheng said, and suddenly the door next to our ears was pulled sharply open.

We panicked. There was no time to think. Daniel sprinted across the corridor like lightning and yanked open the door of a cupboard, which seemed to be full of vacuum cleaners.

Luckily Ms Zheng had turned to say something to Mr Scouter again, giving me exactly one second to dash across the hall and join Daniel in the cramped cupboard, closing the door as quietly as

I could behind me. I waited, holding my breath, for Ms Zheng to find us, pull us out, and give us a hell of a telling-off. But she walked straight down the corridor, her plimsolls squeaking on the lino.

The rest of the teachers filed out of the meeting, sounding like they were leaving the staffroom in both directions. Relief washed over me. We were safe.

Daniel was standing by me at the door, waiting for the all-clear. As soon as the noise of footsteps had died away, I nodded at him, and grasped the knob.

Which was when another pair of hands grabbed us from behind.

5

Tuesday 13 May, 11.15 a.m.

Hanbridge High School cupboard

Daniel jumped so violently that he dislodged a bucket on the shelf beside him, sending it clattering to the concrete floor.

'*nuqDaq 'oH puchpa''e*'!' was what I *think* Daniel yelped.[8] I wondered if he was a little bit odder than I'd thought.

My heart was beating at ninety miles an hour as I turned slowly to see who was in there with us. I really couldn't take any more surprises that day.

---

8 This is a complete guess. He sounded like he was gargling with marbles, to be honest, but it was probably just one of his *Star Trek* references; you'll see what I mean later.

Lydia (who else?) opened her mouth to speak, but then shut it as two more teachers came out of the staffroom talking in low voices. I swivelled back round to peer through the dusty window.

It was Mr Sinclair, the shy-looking geography teacher. '*That* won't come up, surely. Why would the police even ask about it?' he asked his companion, Mrs Sudely, my English teacher. I wondered why they'd been slower to leave the staffroom than the others.

'It shouldn't, it's got nothing to do with what happened to Ollie Baynton. Plus Year Ten won't want to bring any further punishment upon themselves, and they were all off school grounds yesterday evening anyway, so I can't see the police bothering to ask them anything.'

'Yes, but safeguarding procedures must be kept to, and we were rather remiss in our reporting. Perhaps if ...' The conversation faded as they walked away, and we missed the last few words from Mr Sinclair.

'Remiss in their reporting? Safeguarding?' I muttered, somewhat baffled by all the teacher-talk.

'It means they've been slack in their duty to protect us,' explained Lydia. 'But it doesn't matter anyway. I know what they're talking about, and it's not the murder.' She didn't bother to explain further, which was very annoying.

'This is always an excellent spot to overhear the teachers' gossip.' She changed topic, picking the bucket up and placing it back on the shelf. 'I'm on the school newspaper team, and the inside info you can gather from this part of the corridor is quite something.' Lydia looked sideways at Daniel. 'Haven't seen you in here before, though, Daniel.'

I decided then that I didn't want to continue the conversation with this irritating know-it-all. I was also starting to feel hot and bothered in the crowded cupboard. 'We need to go,' I said to Daniel, glancing at my watch. 'Mr Scouter was expecting us outside his office three minutes ago.'

I pushed the door. It didn't budge.

I pushed again.

Daniel pushed too.

I pushed harder.

Nothing. We were trapped. I straightened my blazer in an attempt to win back some dignity.

Lydia didn't seem to be bothered about being stuck.

'I was actually hoping to ask you both for a witness statement,' she said, leaning against the back wall with arms crossed.

'Witness what? Why? None of this has anything to do with you.' I'm not sure why, but I felt like I needed to protect Daniel from her. He was so trembly.

'I'm going for editor of the school newspaper this year. There's an edition out next week and my report on the murder will sweep everything else off the front page! I want your first impressions, details, theories, anything you've got –'

'No,' Daniel cut across. 'It's not funny, Lydia. It was horrible. Mr Baynton's dead – you can't make a . . . *a scoop* out of it.'

I stayed silent, not giving anything away. I didn't want her quoting me.

'But it's the duty of a journalist to report what they hear! Can you just share *something*, anything at all? Any ideas about the possible identity of the murderer, or did you see any clues or find any evidence? I could keep your name out of it, of course. I'd only refer to you as my "source".'

'Well, the teachers have their theories,' Daniel confessed easily. He'd be rubbish in a proper interrogation. 'But they're all stupid.'

Lydia's green eyes flashed in the narrow shaft of light. I heard her click a pen in a businesslike way. 'So I heard! I've been in here a while. Mr Frantock was talking to Miss Black-Dudley in the corridor before you came along. They were all whispery, but I heard them discussing "a believable alibi". That's got to be something to look into.'

I glanced at Daniel and he looked back at me, thoughtful. There was an awful lot going on at this school that I'd never suspected.

However, all this chat wasn't getting us out of the cupboard. I decided to take charge instead of letting Lydia think we were actually having a conversation with her. 'We have no comment. None at all. And we need to go now. Goodbye, Lydia.'

I pushed on the door as hard as I could, both hands. Then Daniel joined me, and we put our shoulders to the flaky painted surface.

To no effect whatsoever.

Daniel made a little whining noise. 'We're stuck!'

I could feel his eyes on me, willing me to have a solution. I looked around. There was no other exit.

Lydia snorted. 'Let's go, before someone overhears your whimpering and we all get in trouble.' She stepped forward and nudged me aside. 'Move out of my way for a second, Jonathan.'

She took a crouching stance and lifted one knee, kicking out her lower leg with surprising speed and agility. It looked like it came right out of an action movie, and was slightly cooler than I'd expected from her.

The door flew open on impact. With lightning reflexes she caught it with her hand before it could crash into the wall. I think she quite enjoyed the looks on our faces.

'See you, then,' she said, and clumped off towards reception. I wondered what she would tell Mrs Fustemann to explain *her* delay in leaving the building. She seemed like the sort of person who could get away with anything.

Daniel and I took all this in silently (we didn't talk about getting stuck in that cupboard ever again, to be honest), before heading down the corridor to the Head's office. Mr Scouter opened the door smartly after Daniel's timid knock.

'Ah! Here you are,' he said, rubbing his hands and smiling warmly. 'No doubt you are both feeling a bit bewildered after the morning you've had. I very much want to talk to you about it, but I need to go over to the PE office now to help the police.' The Head was bouncing on his toes. 'So I want to see you first thing tomorrow morning, right before class, instead. Don't worry, I'll tell your teachers that you won't be at your lessons until quarter past nine.'

I nodded, a bit fazed by his zest, but Daniel looked like he was used to it.

'Before you go!' Mr Scouter ducked back into his office and quickly returned with two sealed envelopes, handing one to each of us. 'Here's a letter that Mrs Fustemann has put together for your parents to reassure them that we're completely on top of this situation. Now, get home safely – and do try to get plenty of sleep tonight. That's how the brain heals, you know!' he said, shutting the door in our faces with as much speed as he'd opened it.

6

Tuesday 13 May, 11.30 a.m.

Hanbridge High School car park

As we passed through the car park at the back of school we didn't say much. We didn't even look at each other. I think we were starting to feel some of that 'bewilderment' Mr Scouter had mentioned.

Suddenly Daniel stopped and pointed at something.

'What's that?' he said.

It was clearly a newspaper, crumpled against the fence behind the science labs. I should have seen it first.

'Good spot! That pathologist said something

about a bit of paper in Mr Baynton's hand, didn't he? And the police asked us if we'd seen any lying around.'

Daniel shrugged. 'Better have a look, then.'

It was a copy of the *Hanbridge Gazette*, the free local news-sheet. It was flapping open in the breeze and there was a bit missing from the top of an inside page.

Daniel bent down and picked it up. 'It might be a clue! We should take it over to the police.'

'Doofus! What about fingerprints?' Had he never seen *CSI* or *NCIS*?[9]

'Oh,' Daniel said and looked at the paper in his hand. 'Bit late now. They can always take mine for elimination, though.'

OK, maybe he had seen one or two episodes.

There were still a couple of SOCOs[10] patiently examining the floorboards in the PE shed as we walked past. POLICE LINE DO NOT CROSS tape was up round the area. I knocked hesitantly on the side of the forensic services van.

---

9 Cop shows from the USA. Basically, a bit like a soap opera, but with gore, so I have to sneakily watch it on Dad's laptop without Mum knowing.

10 SOCO – Scenes of Crime Officer

'Hi, we found this newspaper – across the field. Did you want to take it to see if it's connected to the mur– to the crime?' I said.

Daniel held it out.

An officer took the paper from him and, after no more than a quick glance, chucked it unceremoniously on to the top of the trunk.

I hoped Mr Baynton wasn't still in there.

'So much for preserving forensic evidence,' Daniel muttered quietly.

We turned back and trailed across the field again.

'Daniel, I won't come to yours,' I said. 'I'd prefer – I mean, I'm happy going back to mine and watching TV by myself.'

He looked at me, his deep-brown eyes all shiny. 'I dunno. Maybe you shouldn't be on your own after what we saw, you know?'

I knew. But I didn't want him thinking I was scared or anything.

'Don't be silly! I'll be fine. You get back to your mum, see how she is.'

Then Daniel asked me a weird question.

'Did you know Jonathan Archer is the name of a character in *Star Trek: Enterprise*? He was the captain of the very first warp-five starship that Starfleet sent out. Have you ever seen it?'

I had heard of *Star Trek* but not a series called *Enterprise*. I didn't watch science fiction. I preferred comedy, crime and car shows.

'Was it one of those nineties programmes where everyone wears tight outfits and has big hair?' I guessed.

'Yes, well, noughties not nineties. It's on Netflix, the whole four seasons.' Daniel was starting to look a bit less pale as his enthusiasm for the subject warmed him up. 'Why don't you come and watch it at mine?'

Pants.

Daniel Horsefell might have been the first kid who'd said more than hi to me at this new school, but he was one too many. Plan A for surviving this (hopefully short) time at Hanbridge High was very simple – stay out of trouble, avoid bullies like Tyler Jenkins, and don't do anything noticeable at all. I'd already spoiled my strategy once today by being the mug who found a dead body. And if Lydia had her way, I'd be a minor celebrity by next week.

'No, thanks,' I said firmly.

Daniel's face went all dismal again. I thought about Nanna's empty house, where I could watch what I wanted on the TV and borrow Dad's new laptop without him ever knowing.

Right decision.

We continued on in silence until we got to my turning.

'Bye, then,' I mumbled.

'Yeah, bye,' he replied, not looking up.

I watched him walk a little bit further down the road, his shoulders slumped and his feet hardly leaving the ground. And that stupid, stupid part of me that feels sorry for old-age pensioners and cries at abandoned kittens caught me in the feels.

'OK,' I called, and ran to catch up. 'Maybe I could watch *one* episode with you. As long as we don't – I mean, don't go telling the world that we're besties, or anything.'

Daniel was silent for a moment, digesting this. I felt a twinge of guilt, a bit mean maybe, but it was a necessary Plan A defensive tactic.

Daniel gave me a small smile. 'No problem,' he said. 'We can raid the cupboards for crisps and chocolate. I'm not sure which episode to show you – I guess it makes sense to start at the beginning . . .'

Daniel chatted away, and I followed him, shaking my head. I was an idiot. I didn't want to watch *Star Trek*.

Still, crisps and chocolate.

7

Tuesday 13 May, 11.50 a.m.

Daniel's house

Daniel turned into the front garden of a terraced house on Finney Street. He was just finding the key when the door swung open and a friendly-looking lady with dark hair jumped in surprise at seeing us.

'Daniel! I wasn't expecting to see you here. Your mum's OK, no need to come home in your lunch hour. I've changed her bedding, put a load of washing in and given her some lunch already, as I'm in a bit of a rush.'

Daniel stared at the woman with a very odd look on his face as she swept past. I nudged him and he jolted back into life.

'Lois! Are you . . . are you OK?' he called after her.

Lois was already outside the gate. 'Yeah, course! Why wouldn't I be? I'll see you later, Daniel.'

As she set off down the road, the phone in her hand began buzzing. 'Hello? Yes, this is she. Sorry, I didn't catch that. Inspector Mee . . .?'

Daniel stared at the spot where Lois had been standing, still looking pretty gormless.

'Err . . . are we going in?' I asked.

'Yes, of course. Sorry. Come on in . . . Hi, Mum!' Daniel shouted as he stepped through the front door.

'Oh! Hello, love,' came a voice from upstairs.

Daniel turned from hanging his coat on the banister. 'I'll just go up and check on her.'

I waited in the hall while he took off his shoes and padded up the threadbare steps, wondering if I should take mine off too.

I looked around, to see what I could deduce about Daniel's family from the house. There wasn't much decoration, unless you counted a couple of photos on the walls, and some stiff tea towels drying on the radiator. It was the opposite to Nanna's house – she'd left fuss and frills and fancy patterns everywhere. You could hardly move without dislodging a knick-knack.

I heard murmuring from upstairs and tuned in to listen – it was starting to become a bit of a bad habit. Still, knowledge is power.

'How are you doing, Mum?' Daniel sounded concerned. 'We have a visitor downstairs – Jonathan. He's a new kid at school.'

I couldn't quite catch what his mum said in reply.

'No, well, it was Mrs Fustemann's idea really, but he's a bit shaky after, you know, what happened today . . .'

'What *did* happen?' Daniel's mum raised her voice. 'The old bat just said something about you having witnessed an incident, and Mr Scouter just went on about safeguarding and permission to walk home . . .'

'Oh, nothing to worry about, I'll tell you later. Now, do you want to try coming downstairs or is it a bad day?'

'Not too bad today. So was there an accident? I hope there wasn't any blood, you can't abide that. Were you puking all morning?'

'No, no blood.'

Daniel seemed to be playing the whole murder thing down, for some reason, as he quickly changed the subject. 'I was telling Jonathan all about his

Enterprise character – his surname's Archer! And we thought we might watch a few episodes and chill out for the rest of the afternoon. Why don't you come down and watch it with us? You could do with a bit of company.'

'That *is* true.'

I heard a groan and the sound of mattress springs shifting. It sounded like she needed his help to get up. My Sherlock senses tingled. Not suffering from a simple cold, then.

'Just coming, Jonathan. Make yourself at home in the living room.' Daniel's voice sounded strained as it floated down to where I stood.

I took off my shoes and padded through the door to my left. The living room wasn't much more interesting than the hallway. It was easy to tell which was Daniel's spot – there was a fleece blanket printed with STARFLEET CADET squashed into one corner of the sofa, and a half-eaten bowl of tortilla chips on top.

I finally had a chance to check my phone for messages. Nothing from the group chat. They were probably still in lessons back in Grensham – no dead bodies there. I typed a quick one to catch their attention: **NEWS** DM ME BACK!!

I took a look around.

There were posters on the walls; some looked like old film adverts. *Star Trek II: The Wrath of Khan* had pride of place over the electric fire, and there was a black-and-white one for *Dr. No* on the wall behind the sofa. I'd seen that with Nanna Rosie one Sunday afternoon. Box sets were piled up next to the TV. Clearly television was a serious business in this house.

Daniel's mum shuffled into the room and got settled into the armchair. She was smiling and freckled, but her eyes were dark and baggy and her hair was flat, as if she'd been tossing and turning all night. She was wearing a huge T-shirt with ROCK STAR on the front, and trackie bottoms.

'Pass us the footrest, Daniel,' she said, puffed out. Daniel brought over a weird pile of cushions strapped together with string and made his mum comfy.

I didn't know quite where to look.

Daniel's mum smiled. 'Hi, Jonathan, is it? It's quite an occasion for Daniel to bring a friend home.'

I wanted to say Daniel wasn't, like, an *actual* friend, I just needed a bit of company while Mr Baynton's death was so fresh, that was all. Also, I was promised crisps. But I kept my mouth shut.

Daniel's mum put out a hand to shake mine. 'I'm very pleased to make your acquaintance, Jonathan. My name is Becky and I have a rubbish body. It doesn't do what I want, most of the time.'

8

Tuesday 13 May, 12.20 p.m.

Daniel's house

Daniel went off to the kitchen next door and started crashing around.

'Jonathan – can you help with the crisps?'

I cringed a bit at him using my proper name. I knew he was only trying to be friendly, but no one except Mum called me Jonathan; Jonno, that was me. I'd take Jayden or Kinsey calling me Morticia for the rest of time over *Jonathan*.

I let out a quiet sigh. Plan A wasn't working.

As well as not making friends at school and working myself up to getting detention, at home I had been relying on what Dad called 'surly and uncooperative' behaviour, along with refusing to unpack and being late for every meal. But it didn't really feel like I was doing enough, and I wouldn't be back with my proper friends in Grensham until I'd figured out a decent Plan B.

'Coming,' I called.

I went in and grabbed a bowl of cheesy puffs from the crowded worktop. Before I could take them through to the living room, Daniel put a hand on my arm.

'Don't say too much about what happened at school. I don't want to give her any shocks, it takes so much out of her just coming downstairs.'

I shrugged, and nodded, then went back into the living room. I'd keep the murder part quiet.

Daniel's mum smiled brightly at me as I sat down on the sofa. 'By your accent I'm guessing you're not from round here,' she said. 'Are you in Daniel's class? I haven't heard him mention your name before.'

'Yeah, I used to live in Grensham – Oxfordshire. We moved here at Easter. I know Daniel from my maths group, and we do PE together, too ...' I trailed off awkwardly.

'PE? Is that – is that where this "incident"

happened?' She pulled herself up straighter in her seat, staring at me intently.

'Yes.' I wondered how I could get out of telling her the details, but I couldn't think of anything. 'Mr Baynton was our PE teacher. Didn't Mrs Fustemann tell you?'

Daniel's mum's face lost any trace of pinkness and she grasped the arms of the chair tightly. 'She didn't mention any names, the half-wit.' She rubbed her forehead like it was hurting. 'Daniel! Get in here right now and tell me what happened!'

Daniel ran into the room grasping a second bowl of crisps. 'Sorry, Mum. I thought Lois might want to tell you. She'll be back soon, I expect. We saw her on our way in –'

'How likely is that if her husband's hurt? I should call her – but first, tell me what happened!'

Call me weird but I was *really* curious by now. How did Daniel and his mum know Mr Baynton? Who was this Lois? Was there a big secret? I grabbed some cheesy puffs and opened my ears wide to pay proper attention.

'We . . . we actually found him. He was strangled, I think.' Daniel winced and I figured he was seeing that twisted face in the shadow of the box in the shed, just like I was.

'Strangled!' Her voice went kind of electric. 'Oh my God. He's dead? *Murdered?* I thought there'd been a little accident the way that Fustemann woman explained it!' Daniel's mum pulled her hands through her hair. 'This is awful! If I could just get out of this blasted – what's it called – flipping – *house*, I'd go straight round to Lois's. He wasn't the greatest husband in the world, but it'll still be a horrible shock. Get me the phone, Daniel. I'll call and see if she needs anything.'

I wonder why she can't remember a simple word like 'house'? I thought to myself. Daniel picked up a small, ancient mobile from beside the TV and put it into his mum's trembling hands. Then he signalled at me to follow him into the kitchen again. I'd quite wanted to hear his mum's conversation, to be honest, but there might be more snacks.

The phone started to blip loudly as Daniel's mum made the call. I pulled the living-room door to behind me.

'Sorry about that,' Daniel said. He reached under the counter and pulled out a bottle of Co-op cola. 'I did say. I thought it would be better coming from

Lois when she gets back here, which will probably be as soon as she finds out what's happened to her husband.'

'Who was Mr Baynton?' I asked. 'To you, I mean. And who's Lois?'

Daniel frowned. 'Lois is Mum's best friend and she's sort of, like, her carer. She comes over at lunchtimes to make Mum something to eat and have a gossip. They've known each other forever – since primary school or something – and Mum was her bridesmaid when she got married to Mr Baynton. There's a photo in the hall.'

He took me back out to the narrow space between the stairs and the front door. Up on the wall a much younger-looking version of Daniel's mum was standing next to the pretty, grey-eyed lady I'd seen on the doorstep, who was in a white sleeveless dress. Both of them were smiling.

'Where's Mr Baynton, then?' I asked.

'Oh. Well – Mum never liked him that much, thought he was a self-obsessed louse. So she cut him out of the photo, to "fit the frame". Cheeky, she is.' He looked up at the happy faces. 'He doesn't bother coming to visit Mum, so I only see him at school.' Daniel stopped and swallowed. '*Saw* him.'

The phone blipped again. 'Daniel!' his mum called. 'There's no answer. Can you go over and see if she's OK? It's only round the – you know, nearby – won't take a minute. Jonathan will go with you, won't you, Jonathan? I just need to know she's all right.'

Daniel went into the living room and I heard him say, 'Yes, Mum. Course we will. You sit tight. We'll be back before you can say Federation of Planets!' He came into the hall and reached for his coat.

'You coming?' he asked.

I wasn't sure I had a choice, plus I'd eaten all the cheesy puffs.

Begrudgingly, I put my shoes on.

Tuesday 13 May, 12.45 p.m.

Mr Baynton's house

I was playing it cool in front of Daniel, but secretly I was totally curious to see Mr Baynton's house. It was probably *full* of clues and evidence.

Halfway along Hasdell Road, I glanced at Daniel. 'Will your mum be all right on her own?'

'Yeah, she'll be OK. She's got this thing, it's called chronic fatigue syndrome.'

'What's that, then?'

'About two years ago she got ill – just a virus, the GP said – but it's like she never really got well again. She runs out of energy before she even wakes up in the morning.'

Whoa. 'You mean she can't do anything? Just . . . sleep?'

'Well, she's in pain quite a lot. Her muscles don't have much strength and sometimes her mind gets foggy. Especially when she starts a new medication, then she's more easily confused. But she does what she can.' Daniel gave a small smile. 'She's a good mum.'

We turned the corner on to Ryan Street. There was a police car halfway down the road.

'That's Lois's house! Oh no, are they still in the middle of telling her, d'you think?' Daniel bit his lip and hurried onward.

Now, I reckon if you're in the middle of being told your husband's dead, you might want a bit of privacy. Daniel clearly didn't share my sensitive nature. He marched right up to the front door and rapped three times.

It took a while to get a response. I looked at the cars on the drive – one flashy white BMW and one clapped-out Kia Picanto. Based on what Mr Baynton had been like, I took a wild guess which had been his and which belonged to Lois.

A burly uniformed police constable finally peered out of the door and then down at us. 'Can I help you?'

'Is Lois OK? My mum is her best friend and she wanted us to check she was all right,' Daniel said.

'This is not the time or the place, sonny –' The police officer didn't get any further, because DI Meek appeared behind him and gently shoved him out of the way.

'Hello. What are you two doing here?' she asked. 'I told you to go home, not wander the streets.'

Daniel smiled hopefully up at her. 'Oh, good afternoon again. Actually we *were* at my house, but now we're looking for Mrs Baynton. You see, she's my mum's friend and –'

'I'm afraid Mrs Baynton is currently busy helping us with our enquiries. I'll have to ask you to head home again, boys.' DI Meek's voice was very firm.

Helping with enquiries? I knew what that was code for. LOIS WAS A SUSPECT.

I tried to give Daniel a look, but he didn't seem to want to meet my eye. His shoulders drooped and we turned away. We hadn't even reached the end of the drive when we heard a scuffle behind us.

Lois stood at the Bayntons' front door, face crumpled, grey eyes fierce but full of tears. Her coat was open and her hair a mess. She tried to pull her arm away from DS Norman's grasp.

He walked her towards the police car, followed grimly by DI Meek and the constable.

'Daniel!' she cried as she spotted us.

'Lois? W–what's going on?'

'I didn't do anything! Oh God, what's Becky going to think . . .' She tried to sidestep the open car door. 'I can't believe this is happening! Daniel, tell your mum I'll call her from –'

'Now, now, Mrs Baynton. In you pop,' DS Norman said. He placed a hand on her head to make sure she didn't knock it as he eased her into the car. I didn't know they actually did that in real life.

I was proper shocked, but also weirdly a little disappointed. All my unanswered questions about the case drained away.

The police had their woman.

The investigation was already over.

Tuesday 13 May, 1.15 p.m.

Daniel's house

I stood by the living-room door, back at Daniel's house, listening to him fuss over his mum. I could have gone home already, but I was kind of into the drama. It was almost like being in an episode of *Midsomer Murders*.[11]

I regretted being so bloody nosy as soon as Daniel told his mum what had happened. She tried to get up out of her chair, almost tripping over that weird footstool thing. Her face was shiny with the effort.

11 Cosy British crime drama that's been on TV for what feels like centuries. One of Nanna's favourite watches on a soggy winter afternoon.

'Mum, calm down. You know it'll give you a flare-up.' Daniel guided her gently back into her seat.

'But how can they think Lois would do something like that? She's the . . . best, no . . . *gentlest* person I know!'

'Of course she didn't do it – it's ridiculous. They'll soon figure that out, though. Won't they?' Daniel looked over at me, sounding like he really needed the answer. 'I heard Mr Frantock mention her name at school, but I didn't think anyone would really believe Lois was involved.'

So *that* was why he started listening at the door of the staffroom! I held in a grunt of satisfaction at solving a little bit of the mystery.

Daniel's mum fumbled for a tissue, patting it over her blotchy face.

'We'll call a solicitor! She'll have a . . . what's-it-called, you know? Alibi. Evidence to show she couldn't have done it. It'll be OK, you'll see, it'll be fine . . .'

I felt awkward listening to all this, seeing Becky so upset, even though it was extremely interesting.

I started to back out of the door. 'Look, Mrs . . . Becky . . . I can see I'm here at a difficult time, so I'm just gonna go home. I'll see you tomorrow, Daniel.'

'Jonathan – no, hang on. Don't go.' Daniel

clutched at my arm, pulling me into the hallway. 'We need your help.' He glanced through the door frame at his mum, who was leaning back in her chair staring at the ceiling, trying not to cry.

'Come upstairs,' he said.

I followed him up, taking a quick glance at my phone on the way. Still nothing in the group chat. *How come everyone's so quiet all of a sudden?* Some days there could be sixteen messages before morning break.

Daniel's room was even smaller than Max's room at Nanna's old house – Mum calls it a box room, probably because it's not much bigger than an Amazon delivery. Nanna used to do her ironing in there. It still smells a bit Febreze-y.

There was clutter everywhere. On a hook was a top hat with scarves tumbling out of it, and hanging on the wardrobe door a full Starfleet uniform with blue shoulders. Every inch of Daniel's walls was papered with photos, posters, even a couple of vinyl record sleeves. He had loads of group shots of the *Star Trek* cast too, and those were just the pics I vaguely recognized.

'Who's this?' I pointed to a grainy black-and-white photo of a young man in a tuxedo.

'That's Bix Beiderbecke, this amazing jazz trumpet player who made music sound like bullets from a bell.' Daniel ran his fingers through his short blonde hair. 'But that's not important! Lois can't go to prison. She just can't – Mum needs her. *I* need her. And there's no way she'd kill anyone, ever.'

I felt confused at this. 'OK, but what on earth do you expect me to do?' I asked.

Daniel dropped his hands by his sides. 'You've got to help me find out who *did* do it,' he said.

I snorted.

'You're kidding. How on earth are *we* going to find anything out? If your mum's mate's been arrested, the police will have a good reason, won't they?' I couldn't really imagine Mrs Baynton as a murderer, but this was real life and the police knew their stuff. Perhaps if this was a murder mystery, it'd be different.

Daniel turned to look at his shelves, crowded with *Doctor Who* paperbacks and assorted knick-knacks, and picked up a pack of playing cards.

'Not necessarily,' he muttered, riffling the cards through his fingers really fast. 'They just pick the most obvious person to start with, don't they? Husbands and wives are always the prime suspects.'

'Well, she could have been ready to skip off to Cuba for all we know. She did say she was in a rush earlier.' I sat on the bed, staring up at Daniel. 'Anyway, what did you mean when you said *you* need her?'

Daniel shuffled the cards again. 'OK, if I tell you – do you swear never to repeat it to a living soul?'

'I swear. Who would I tell anyway? I'm just the new boy, remember.'

'Cool. Thanks. So . . .' He took a deep breath and put down the cards. 'Mum's illness is more or less permanent, as I said. But what you don't know is that she's got this, like . . . paranoia. She overheard the nurses chatting about her, when she first got ill. They said if she got worse she might not be capable of caring for a child by herself.'

'Ah,' I murmured. What else could I say? This was deep stuff.

'Ever since then, Mum's worried. Worried a lot. And it's down to me to keep her calm. And if she thought someone – like social services – was coming to take me away from her . . . well. She might not be able to take it.' Daniel took a deep breath, his chin quivering. 'Lois works a lot in the evenings, you see, cos she's a yoga teacher. But she comes here during the day, *every* day, no pay or anything, just to keep

Mum company and make sure she's OK. She's so much better when she's calm. So Mum *needs* Lois, and so do I.'

I nodded slowly. 'So if Lois gets put in prison – your mum thinks social services will be round for you?' I asked.

Daniel nodded, those Bambi eyes boring into me. 'And then ... her worst fear might actually come true.'

I could see his point, at last.

'What do you need *me* for, though?' I still wasn't sure what Daniel thought I could achieve. Sure, I loved a murder mystery but I was just a normal almost-teenager, trying to make it back to his old life, not particularly clever or brave or confident. Oh yeah – and I didn't know anyone or anything in this poxy town.

'Whatever they've got on Lois, we have to disprove it, Jonathan, or find out who really did it. Mum won't be able to afford a solicitor. We'll have to do this by ourselves.'

11

Tuesday 13 May, 1.30 p.m.

Daniel's house

I stayed still, organizing my thoughts. I was damn-straight not going to tell him that my heart was starting to pound and I was getting that feeling, you know, when the world seems to go from black and white to colour and all your hairs stand up.

A brilliant idea had started to blossom in my mind. Finding a dead body at my new school was a pretty rubbish way to start. But actually getting mixed up in the case? I was bound to get into deep, deep trouble for that. I didn't have to hang out with Daniel forever, just help him a bit. We would no doubt get into some big FAT trouble, and I'd earn enough detentions to convince Mum and Dad that moving to Hanbridge was a bad thing for us. Then I could concentrate on packing up and getting back to my *proper* mates.

This was it! Plan B! It couldn't fail!

Could it?

'Look, I'm not promising anything.' I tried to sound all casual. 'I mean, I've never even done an investigation before. Who's going to tell two school kids anything?'

'I don't know.' Daniel frowned in concentration, fiddling with a half-finished model spaceship made of tiny bits of moulded plastic.

I thought back to Nanna Rosie's murder-mystery books. 'OK, well, we'll need to check out motives, means and opportunities. Maybe you could start by making a list of people who might have had a reason to want Mr Baynton out of the way? Like the teachers were saying.'

Daniel stayed focused on the spaceship. 'I suppose there's Gavin.'

'Who's Gavin?' I asked.

Daniel shrugged. 'He used to be Mr B's best friend. He was best man at their wedding and everything. In fact, I think he was on the other half of that photo downstairs, the half Mum threw out. But Lois mentioned they'd had a big fight – not long ago – which nearly ended in a punch-up.'

'Well, that's a start. Can you get more out of your mum about it?'

'OK, I'll try.' Daniel stopped fiddling with the model spaceship and looked straight at me. 'Thanks, Jonathan. I really – I don't know what else to do. Just – please don't say anything about Mum to anyone at school. It's my business and I definitely don't want anyone getting on my case about it.'

I grunted in reply. I needed to give my brain a break. It felt like four million years since I'd agreed to come to this house and watch *Enterprise*. 'Right,' I said. 'Let's go get some snacks and you can show me this Captain Archer thing.'

Back in the living room, Daniel's mum was still staring into space, tapping the phone against the chair arm.

'I've just rung a couple of solicitors. The fees are completely stupid. So we're going to have to rely on the . . . the legal place . . . the *court* to assign someone to Lois's case.'

Daniel went over and took the phone off her. 'We've been trying to think of anyone else who might have had a motive. What about Gav?'

Daniel's mum sat up a little straighter. 'Ooh, I hadn't thought . . . I mean, I don't know when Lois last saw him. I'll try and find out what he and Ollie had that fight about, shall I, and where he's been since?'

'Not now, Mum. You look pooped. Why don't you watch TV with us, and I'll bring you a sandwich? Lois will be fine. They'll have to let her go soon. Just try and rest for a bit.'

Daniel made a good mother hen. His mum nodded and sank back into the saggy chair, but her under-eyes were dark and her hands trembled.

Daniel put *Enterprise* on. It was OK, actually. We watched three episodes and I started to get into it. The captain, Archer, was pretty badass. He didn't let the Vulcans get away with keeping secret information from the humans.

While Daniel and his mum were focused on the telly, I finally got the chance to go on the group chat and tell them how I found a body and everything. But all I got was a shocked-face emoji off Jayden and, briefly, a three dot 'typing' symbol off Georgia, which didn't turn into a message.

66

I sank down into the sofa – they were losing interest in me already! The sooner I got myself in some proper trouble, the sooner I'd be back with my real mates.

They wouldn't be able to forget about me then.

12

Tuesday 13 May, 6.30 p.m.

Nanna Rosie's house

I got 'home' before Mum and Dad did that afternoon.

Mrs Fustemann had done the same job on them as she'd done to Daniel's mum – they had no idea what had actually happened, just that there had been an 'incident' that meant the school had to shut early. Dad tried to ask about it when he got in, but I just walked past him and headed up to my room. I didn't give him the envelope from Mr Scouter – that had gone in a bin next to a bus stop – and I didn't want him thinking I was in a chatty mood.

I wanted a quiet evening to dream about how this investigation might rattle him and Mum to the point of going back to Grensham.

But then Dad watched the news while Mum was putting Max to bed. Mr Baynton and the school were all over the local bulletin.

He came upstairs in his slippers, left knee creaking with every step. His head poked round the door as I lay on my bed, trying to ignore the annoying sounds of Max's bath time and concentrate on one of Nanna Rosie's old Poirot books.

'They've just said on the news there were two boys who found this body. That was what Mrs Fustyface meant when she said you'd been involved in an incident, wasn't it?' Dad stared down at me like I was a Klingon.[12] 'And you didn't think it was important to tell us?' He looked round at Nanna's revolting patterned wallpaper. I'd been given her best guest room, and it hadn't been redecorated since 1985.

'Are you OK?' he asked, after a few moments.

---

12 I'd discovered that afternoon that Klingons are a proud warrior species in *Star Trek* who value honour and combat. They don't always get on well with humans. They're Daniel's favourite aliens.

I shrugged, not lifting my eyes from my book. 'Well, it was horrible, but I only saw him for a second. You do that all the time –'

'Yes, that's one of the good things about working at an undertaker's, you're never particularly surprised to see a corpse.' He came into the room and sat on the end of my bed. 'But it's not normal, Jonathan, finding a murdered teacher at school. Are they getting you some counselling?'

I sighed. 'We've got to see Mr Scouter about it tomorrow.' Now seemed a good time to start planting the idea I was in trouble. 'And the police might want to talk to me again, to take a statement.'

'The police? What do they think *you* know? You're not likely to have spotted anything they didn't.'

Typical. 'Kids are much sharper-eyed than adults, Dad, everyone knows that.'

He ignored my cranky tone of voice. 'Well, I don't know about that, but what I do know is I'm not going to tell your mother because she'd only worry and probably want you to move schools again, and we've just spent a big wad of cash on your new uniform. So if you're sure you're OK, then let's keep this between ourselves. But I want you to *talk* to me if you are feeling upset, yes?' He stood up and started to move back towards the door. 'I'm going to go and say goodnight to Max, so I'll leave you to your book.'

Mum worrying wasn't anything new, but I did kick myself. I'd been so busy thinking of this complicated Plan B to scare Mum and Dad into moving back to Grensham that I'd not seen the obvious. Perhaps me finding Mr Baynton was all it would take to convince her? Dad clearly wasn't going to bite, but if Mum believed Hanbridge was a dangerous place, she might insist we go back?

After dinner, I waited in my room until Mum and Dad were fully absorbed in their Netflix show (old people can't get enough of boring period dramas), then I crept downstairs to the kitchen and tuned the radio to the local station. Mum always listened to the radio in the morning, and hopefully when she switched it on first thing there'd be a news report on Mr Baynton's murder.

I'd have to call this Plan B.5, or something.

My phone started vibrating as I crept back up the stairs. I must have been more on edge than I realized, cos I jumped a mile. I didn't recognize the number but I guessed straightaway it was Daniel. I'd given him mine before I left his house, in case anything happened, but hadn't added him to my contacts. Didn't think there was much point if I wasn't staying at Hanbridge long.

'Hi,' I said. 'What's up?'

Daniel's voice was whispery and distorted. I guessed he was using that ancient mobile again. 'Hi, Jonathan. So I've had an idea. Are you up for ... I don't know, maybe this won't be any use ...'

'I'll tell you if I think it's pointless,' I said. 'But you might as well spit it out, now you've called.'

'OK.' Daniel's voice crackled in my ear. 'I don't know why I didn't think of this earlier – I've got a spare key. For Lois's house. Maybe we could go over there and ... take a look around? Just to see if there's anything that might give us a clue as to why Mr Baynton might have been ... you know.'

I knew. 'Do you mean tomorrow? Like, before school?'

'Nooo. I was sort of thinking ... now? There won't be any police there at night, and we can avoid being spotted by the neighbours now it's dark. I'll make sure Mum's comfy and give her her medicine, she won't notice I've gone if we're quick about it.'

I looked at the clock – fairly late, 9.20 p.m. It

was, no doubt about it, *very* bad behaviour to sneak out of the house at night and break into a teacher's house, even if Daniel did have a key. Mum and Dad would go SPARE.

That made my mind up for me.

'Sure! Why not. Where do you want to meet?'

'Corner of my road? Be there in ten minutes. Wear dark stuff and bring a little torch if you've got one. We'll need to be careful.'

'OK. See you there.' I put the phone down and looked around. I had changed into my joggers when I got home from Daniel's, and all I needed was an extra hoodie over my grey sweater. I'd have to use the light on my phone as a torch. I shoved it into my pocket, grabbed my house keys, and went down the stairs on my tiptoes.

Mum and Dad were still huddled up watching TV on the sofa as I slid into the kitchen and picked up the rubber gloves by the sink. Not quite SOCO-grade equipment, but they'd have to do.

Back in the hall, I turned the catch slowly on the front door and slipped through the tiniest gap possible. I held my breath as I pulled the handle softly closed. If I was going to get caught, I'd prefer it to be on the way back in. That'd be loads worse.

I ran along the road towards Daniel's, hoping I wouldn't bump into anyone. This was later than I'd been out on my own, and it was a strange town.

And if Daniel was right, and Lois was in fact innocent, that meant the real murderer was still out there.

13

Tuesday 13 May, 9.25 p.m.

Near Lois Baynton's house

I slowed down and walked the last bit, not wanting to look scared when I met Daniel. He was already there waiting for me as I strolled towards the corner.

'You made it! Thank you.' Daniel gave me a nervous smile. 'Are you ready? I've got the key.'

'You do know it might be a crime scene? All locked up and impossible to access?' I'd only thought of this two seconds before, but he didn't need to know that.

'Oh. Yeah.' Daniel looked glum in the light from the nearest lamp-post. 'We might as well try, though.'

'Now we're here,' I agreed.

We walked casually down Hasdell Road then turned into Ryan Street, looking around, left and right, before we slipped into the Bayntons' front drive, past the cars. The front door was firmly shut but there was no sign of any extra police security.

Daniel pulled a small bunch of keys from his pocket, blinged up with a shiny Bristol Rovers keyring. 'Lois gave me these so I could water her tomatoes when they went away last summer,' he explained.

The lock clicked satisfyingly as he turned the key. We stepped into the dark hallway and shut the door behind us.

Daniel already had his torch out, but before he could illuminate anything I took a step and tripped over, face first on to the carpet.

'Ow!' I said, too loudly.

'Shhhhhhh!' Daniel's torch beam swung across my prone body and lit up a wheely suitcase, standing forlornly near the doormat. 'What's this?' He examined it close up while I struggled to my feet and rubbed my carpet-burned nose.

'It's a suitcase, obviously. It might be important, but let's look around first, we can open it in a bit if there's nothing else to see.' I suddenly didn't feel like hanging about, to be honest. The shock of the fall had shaken loose any sense of mischief I'd had when I left my house.

'Living room,' Daniel whispered, and indicated the dark opening on our right. I got my phone out before I moved. The torch showed me a neat room with light curtains and a tartan sofa. I went over to the bookcase and had a look. Mostly sports biographies, romances and yoga manuals.

'This is where they keep all their paperwork, look,' Daniel said. He was at an antique-looking writing desk in one corner, the kind with a flap at the top and a drawer underneath.

'Nice,' I replied. We'd taken a similar one from Nanna's house to the tip before we'd unloaded our boxes from the removal van into her house. 'Why don't you look through that and I'll go to the kitchen – there might be something there and we'll waste time if we stick together.'

I put on the rubber gloves, went back out into the hall and into the room at the end. It was a small kitchen with slightly clapped-out cupboards and a dripping tap. Stuck on the fridge with magnets was a monthly calendar, filled in with two different styles of handwriting, and on one work surface was a load of junk mail. Stacked next to the pile of leaflets (pizza, double glazing, all the usual rubbish) were some pink and grey flyers.

Yoga with Lois!
Movement, deep relaxation and breathing.
Suitable for all ages and abilities.
7–8 p.m. Tuesdays and Thursdays in the
main hall at Hanbridge High School.

If I remembered right what Mr Scouter had said, this meant there was a strong chance that Lois had an access pass to the school! I filed it away in my brain under 'useful information'.

I brought my torch up to look at the calendar. May. Lois's column had her yoga classes listed on regular dates, along with 'Beck' written against every morning. She really was committed to Daniel's mum, I'll say that for her.

The other column was marked 'Ollie' and most of the entries were on the weekends. I deduced that he was busy at school during the week. His handwriting was unreadably bad, so I used my phone camera to take a quick snapshot, but it was so dark the flash bleached the whole thing out.

There wasn't anything else interesting in the kitchen, except for a biscuit tin (I had just enough self-control not to open it). I went back to the living room to find Daniel, but it was completely empty.

I was just about to creep out to look upstairs for him when a quiet voice from the depths of the gloom made me jump, with my heart in my mouth.

'It's just Lois's bills and invoices in here. Mr Baynton must have kept his stuff somewhere else.'

It turned out he was sitting on the floor on the other side of the armchair, leafing through a pile of paperwork. I closed my eyes for a second to calm myself.

I thought about my parents – everything important they had was kept together, albeit higgledy-piggledy, mixed up in a metal filing box under the stairs. Every couple of years they got it out and had a big shredding party.

'That's a bit weird – why would they keep their paperwork separate?' I thought aloud.

'Maybe he's hidden it for a reason,' Daniel said, shining his torch up under his chin. 'Maybe there's something he didn't want Lois to find out about?'

'Hmmm, maybe,' I said. 'There might be more upstairs. There's certainly nothing in the kitchen.'

I led the way up, hoping the stairs weren't too creaky. Who knows what the neighbours might do if they heard us?

There were three rooms at the top of the stairs. I could see a bit of shower curtain showing through the crack of one of the doors, so I ignored that one. Mr Baynton wasn't going to keep paperwork in the bathroom. The door on the left was half open; there was a frilly floral duvet visible on a double bed, with a chest of drawers next to it supporting a single cream lamp. Based on what I'd seen of Mr Baynton's swanky get-up, I guessed this was Lois's taste.

Daniel pushed open the third door to reveal what looked like a fully kitted-out home gym. A big, shiny machine, like ones you'd see in a proper leisure centre, with weights hanging off it to train every part of the body, filled more than half the room. There were also some kettlebells and a rowing machine taking up more floor space, but in one corner, looking rather out of place, stood a short, grey filing cabinet.

'Whoa,' I said. 'No room for yoga in here.'

'Nah,' said Daniel, flashing his torch around to check it all out. 'He was more into team sports where people run around and throw things at each other.'

'Come on, let's try that,' I said, pointing at the filing cabinet.

It was locked, of course. Neither of us were brave enough to tug the top drawer very hard, in case we made a noise. I checked my watch – it was already ten to ten.

'His keys must be somewhere. Maybe he kept them in their room – in the bedside table or something?' I whispered.

Once we actually got into the Bayntons' bedroom, I got the proper shivers. On the wall next to us was a wardrobe and another chest of drawers, this one with a large mirror and several different fancy brands of aftershave and deodorant on top.

'I guess that one's Mr Baynton's,' I said.

We both stood there for a few seconds, neither one of us keen to touch a dead man's belongings.

I took a deep breath in and let it out in a long *oooooofff*. 'OK. I'll look in the wardrobe, and you start on the drawers.'

'No problem, Captain,' Daniel said, with a little salute.

My phone torch revealed a lot of clothes in that wardrobe. Shirts, most of them expensive ones by the look, and several swish trousers and jackets.

There were a few designer tracksuits too. I don't know where he wore them all – not in school, anyway. There were a few summery dresses squashed at one end of the rail.

I felt in the pockets of all the sports jackets and came up empty, apart from a couple of half-finished packs of chewing gum. I crouched down and started opening shoe boxes – there were piles of them, all full of Nikes, and a couple of pairs of Gucci loafers. No keys anywhere.

I reached to the back of the wardrobe and felt around, hoping I wasn't going to end up in Narnia. There was nothing but smooth, warm wood.

'No luck here, Daniel,' I said, making him flinch a little as I clicked the wardrobe door shut.

'Crud. I've just got the bottom drawer to go –'

BRRRRRRRR! We both leaped a mile as a loud ringtone, right under our noses, shattered the silence.

Tuesday 13 May, 10.00 p.m.

Lois Baynton's house

Daniel's white face stared up at mine, his mouth open in shock.

'It's yours! Shut it up, quick!' I yelped. I admit, I lost my cool at that moment.

Daniel fumbled in his jeans and pulled out the ancient mobile. UNKNOWN CALLER was flashing on the small screen. He pressed the green icon with a shaking finger and held the phone up to his ear. 'Hello? Who is this?'

I heard the reply, even over the rapid thumping of my heart. 'Daniel, it's Lois, I'm still at the police station.'

Daniel looked up and beckoned me to put my head next to his, so I could listen too.

'Are you alright?' Daniel said, keeping his voice low. 'Are they letting you go now? Do you need me to book you a taxi?'

'Oh, love. No, not exactly. You're going to have to break this to your mum very gently – that's why I'm calling you, not her.'

Daniel's body went absolutely still. 'So – they're keeping you for a while longer?'

'Daniel, they're preparing the charge sheet. This is my one call, to let someone know where I am. Things don't look great, even though I swear to you – on my mother's grave – that I'm innocent.'

'I know you are! I just can't believe this is happening. Why do they think it was you?'

'I've got to be quick – the custody sergeant is telling me to get off the phone. The neighbours heard me and Ollie having one of our rows late yesterday afternoon, and he stomped off in a foul temper. So I followed him to school to try and sort it out, but Mrs Fustemann stopped me at the office. When he didn't come home last night, I decided I'd finally had enough, so I started packing to move out.' Lois's breath rasped in our ears. 'When the police turned up this morning, there I was with a suitcase ready to leave. I hadn't reported him missing, I had no alibi, and they'd been looking through his phone and seen my texts, saying how much I hated him and was going to make him sorry –'

'But that's just circumstantial!' The words left Daniel's lips in a rush.

'It seems to be a good enough motive for them. Look, Daniel, I must go now. Please break this very carefully to Becky, and see if you can find anyone to pop in on her tomorrow. I'm so sorry, she's not going to manage well, is she . . .?'

'Don't worry, Lois. I'll look after her. You just take care of yourself –'

The phone blipped as Lois put down the receiver at her end.

My mind was all over the place. She sounded so sincere, but was she really? If the police thought they had enough to charge her, there must be more to it than she had said. Lois's yoga flyer told me as much: Mr Scouter said that people who ran evening classes at school had security access passes, so she *could* have been there.

I had to pull myself together; Daniel was a mess. I think he'd been secretly clinging to the hope that it was all going to be OK without the need for us to get involved.

'Come on, Daniel. Let's get home – we can try again tomorrow.'

'*No.*' Daniel's moist eyes caught mine in the dimming light of his torch, which he was holding shakily. 'It's even more important to find evidence now. We've got to prove them wrong!' He knelt on the floor and dragged open the last drawer.

I peered over his shoulder. It was full of small containers, cufflink boxes and sunglasses cases, coiled-up belts and, in one corner, a stack of brand-new baseball caps.

'Get opening,' he said. 'This'd be the place to hide a key, I'm sure of it.'

There was no point in arguing, no matter how much I wanted to. Daniel's mind was made up, and I couldn't bring myself to leave him there alone. We both silently got stuck in; box after box opened, contents examined and then put back into the drawer.

'Here!' It was me who found it, a bunch of three identical keys in an empty watch box marked

TAG HEUER.[13] There was a shiny gold credit card in there too. Daniel picked it up and turned it over.

We scrambled up and took ourselves into the gym room.

Daniel was still a bit wobbly so I did the honours. Inside the top drawer was a series of plastic folders, all marked in the same terrible handwriting I'd seen on the calendar downstairs.

'Hedge ... no, Health Ins ... sewer ... ants? House ... This one, Bank Statements, you take that,' I said to Daniel, passing him the file.

I picked out a notebook from the bottom of the drawer. It had been underneath all the folders, and I got a tingle in my fingers when I picked it up. You have a certain level of intuition when you've read the amount of detective stories I have.

I opened it to a page marked up with columns, each one filled in with a mix of figures and letters. Was it a code? It looked more like shorthand, and it didn't ring any bells with me. The first column might refer to dates, but otherwise I was stumped.

13 A fancy brand of watch I'd seen advertised in some of Mum's high-end magazines.

The last few entries were:

2/4	BTVFP	50	3/1	150
3/4	GCVSG	70	7/2	245
10/4	CRVGC	120	9/1	1080
11/4	SLVBC	85	6/1	510

'Look!' Daniel waved a piece of paper under my nose, derailing my train of thought. 'He's got a bank account with nothing but small-to-medium sized payments going in. Definitely not his monthly salary from school. And he just uses the money to pay off a credit card account. Maybe this gold card . . . Yes, the long number matches. That's got to be worth knowing. Maybe it's to do with some dodgy plot he was caught up in?'

'Maybe.' I shrugged. He could be right, but I was so tired, suddenly, that I felt incapable of guessing what it might mean. 'What do you want to do with it? Because, like, it's gone ten and it's been a hell of a day, Daniel.'

Daniel shrugged. 'I don't really know. We could take it to the police . . . but it might not be enough to go on, and we'd be in trouble for sneaking in here.' He sighed. 'Tell you what, I'll take it all home with me. We might find more clues elsewhere and if we can bring all the evidence to the police in one go it'll be better, won't it?'

I passed the notebook to Daniel and he tucked it under his jumper with the folder.

We got out quickly, not bothering to look inside Lois's suitcase – she'd told us what that was for on the phone. It was cold and very dark outside, and both our faces gleamed yellow under the streetlight.

'See you tomorrow, then,' I said as we reached the corner.

'Thanks for coming, Jonathan. I hope you get back in without getting caught,' Daniel whispered.

But even though getting caught was exactly what I wanted, I was as quiet as a fieldmouse getting in and creeping up to bed. I just felt too knackered and shaky to make lots of noise and deal with the fall-out of being discovered. Instead, I slid into my room and, even with Dad's loud snores echoing contentedly through the house, I fell asleep almost as soon as my head hit the pillow.

Wednesday 14 May, 8.05 a.m.

Nanna's house

The next morning I dragged myself out of bed and went downstairs. I picked up the *Bristol Post* from the doormat on the way into the kitchen, where Mum and Max were already up and eating breakfast. The radio was off, and they had Max's annoying nursery-rhyme CD playing instead.

'Maximilian,' I called. He looked over and grinned at me with his mouth full of Weetabix. I grinned back. He was disgusting, but cute.

'Morning, *Knuddelbär*.' Mum didn't really notice me, her focus on Max's breakfast as she tried to prevent him from turning the cereal bowl upside down. 'What lessons do you have today?'

I arranged the paper carefully so that the headline – TEACHER FOUND MURDERED AT HANBRIDGE HIGH – was face-up on the table. I put a bit of attitude into my voice to try and get her attention.

'History, maths, RE; not that I care.'

'Don't be rude! Have you made any new friends yet? You know you cannot sit back and expect the people to come to you. You must be friendly!'

Yeah, right! Like it isn't your fault I've got no mates? I felt the fire in my belly, the one that had been burning since January, start to flicker and flame. Last time I had to make new friends was in Reception class, and I'd kept the same ones ever since. The Grensham gang were like family and, until we moved here, I spoke to them almost every day. Since we'd been in Hanbridge my phone had only rung that one time, last night, and that was Daniel. I pushed the uneasy feeling to the back of my mind.

'I have made a friend, sort of,' I said, hoping she would look up and see the paper.

She didn't. She watched Max as he spooned a lump of mush in the general direction of his mouth.

'Such excellent news. Well done! Who is it?'

'Daniel. He does PE with me. He lives just down the road. He was there yesterday when we found . . .' I coughed in a deliberate way and nudged the paper on the table. Mum turned away from Max and her eyes fell across the headline.

'When you . . . *Was in aller Welt?*'[14]

The next ten minutes were pretty full on. This easy version of the plan (B.5) did not entirely work. Mum went ballistic, but mostly at me for not telling her about the body earlier. She didn't so much as mention going back to Grensham.

'This is terrible, Jonathan! You must not keep such things from your parents, we have the right to know when you have been exposed to such traumas! I'm going to telephone the school today and give them pieces of my mind, I can tell you –'

'Mum! You can't. Haven't you ruined my life enough?' I needed to kick my attitude up a notch if I was going to get her thinking the right way.

'Do not speak to me that way! We are having some serious issues with your behaviour, young man. I will not tolerate it!'

14 Mum drops into German when she's excited or stressed. This phrase means 'What on earth . . .?'

I reckon I only got out of there alive because I had school to go to, but she swore she'd be outside the gates to meet me and make sure I got home safely. Could she be more embarrassing? I might as well have stuck a badge on my blazer saying LOSER in bright red letters.

Telling her about the body hadn't done enough, but at least I could focus on full-fat Plan B now: get completely involved in solving the crime, and properly scaring Mum and Dad into moving us back to Grensham.

***

When I turned up at the school office, Lydia Strong was hanging around in the foyer, pretending to tie her shoelaces. I walked past like I hadn't noticed her.

Inside, Mrs Fustemann was sitting at her massive and obsessively neat desk in the middle of the room. She pointed towards some stained chairs in the corner.

'Sit quietly and wait,' she said, glaring at me. 'Mr Scouter will be with you when he's ready. Don't waste his time, either of you. He has a great deal to cope with at present.'

Daniel was already there, looking weary. I could feel the gazes of the other office staff as they leaned around their partitions to check us out.

The body finders.

A younger woman wearing a bright blue scarf came right out of her little nook and stared at us while she got a drink of water from the cooler.

'Miss Hussam! Get back to your desk.' Mrs Fustemann wasn't having any of it.

'That's Zaara Hussam. She was in Year Eleven last year, but then she got unlucky – took a job as Mrs Fustemann's apprentice,' Daniel murmured.

Mrs Fustemann's phone rang and she picked up, glaring at Zaara's retreating back. 'Hanbridge High, how may I help you?'

I watched with interest as her face went red.

'No, Mr Scouter will *not* be making any statements to the press at this time. He is a very busy man. Please stop ringing – we will let you know when we have something to say!' She slammed down the receiver.

The inner door to Mr Scouter's office opened, and there he was, green stripy tie slightly crooked, moustache taking over his face. 'Come in, Mr Horsefell, Mr Archer, come in. Sorry to keep you waiting. Just getting some paperwork ready for my lovely wife – ah, there you are, dear.'

The office door had swung wide open.

'Hi, Andrew,' said the tall and smartly dressed lady who'd opened it. 'Have you got those accounts? I can't stop long, I'm on my way out for coffee.'

'They're here. Thank you for stopping by. We're so lucky to have your help balancing the books.'

Mrs Fustemann gave an epic snort and covered it up with a cough. I looked straight ahead and wondered if she was jealous of the 'lovely wife'. She certainly seemed keen on being the one to look after Mr Scouter's comfort and happiness.

'Are you quite well, Millie?' asked Mrs Scouter, eyes wide.

'Perfectly, thank you,' Mrs Fustemann bit back like a shark. She was in a terrible mood.

'Are these the poor boys you were telling me about?' Mrs Scouter asked her husband.

'Yes, indeed. Terrible business,' agreed Mr Scouter.

Mrs Fustemann snorted again. I wondered why she was being so obvious – most people wouldn't dare be rude to their boss's wife.

'Do take care of them, won't you,' Mrs Scouter said, ignoring Mrs Fustemann and smiling kindly at us.

'Of course. That is why they're here.' Mr Scouter pushed us gently into his room before handing a sheaf of papers to Mrs Scouter.

I wished I was there for a better reason. Getting expelled in my first fortnight would have been an excellent strategy. Even a few days of detention would have done. Unfortunately, the bad attitude I could easily summon up around Mum and Dad was harder to do around other adults, especially senior staff. An unhelpful respect for authority kept kicking in.

'Now, have a seat.' Mr Scouter gestured to the low-slung chairs in the middle of the room. 'Mrs Fustemann has kindly got some squash and biscuits in. It's only fruit shortcake, I'm afraid – chocolate digestives are a little out of our price range these days.'

Daniel and I sat down. 'Thanks, sir,' we both murmured and took a stale biscuit from the coffee table beside us.

Mr Scouter's office was a mess, unlike Mrs Fustemann's military precision outside. He had half-open filing cabinets and half-eaten doughnuts and half-drunk cups of coffee. I wondered if he ever finished anything he started.

'So. We were going to talk about your rather unpleasant experience yesterday. Would you mind telling me what happened? I know you're going to need to tell the police later, but it might be sensible to talk it through here and get the facts straight first.'

I looked at Daniel. 'Well, we were ready for PE, first period, and Mr Baynton hadn't arrived yet . . .'

'We were all outside getting cold and someone said to go and get the footballs – not sure who it was.' It was Tyler Jenkins, but not even Daniel was fool enough to grass him up. 'Jonathan and I were closest, so we tried the equipment shed door . . .'

'It wasn't locked, so we went in. Couldn't see the footballs, just tennis balls and hockey sticks, so I opened the trunk . . .' I hesitated. 'And saw him. I closed the box back up, straight away, because Daniel was a bit –'

'I threw up, sir.' Daniel shuddered slightly. 'Sick as a crewman on their first spaceflight.'[15]

'And I stood guard until you came, Mr Scouter.' I shrugged. 'You know the rest.'

---

15 I was starting to get the impression that Daniel genuinely believed he was a member of Starfleet.

'I see.' Mr Scouter looked at us both sympathetically. 'And how do you feel now? It is certainly not a sight we would want you to be exposed to. Have you had any anxiety since? Bad dreams last night?'

Daniel shrugged.

'I didn't dream, sir,' I said. And I hadn't, I'd been out like a light after our little adventure.

'Can we ask you something, sir?' asked Daniel.

He sat up a bit and leaned towards Mr Scouter (who was eating his fifth biscuit and was covered in crumbs).

'We can't help wondering. Clearly Mr Baynton was murdered, and we wondered why, sir? Had he been threatened or anything? Or is there, like, a maniac on the loose in Hanbridge?'

Daniel did his Bambi thing again, and I was kind of impressed. Maybe he's not as daffy as he pretends to be.

Mr Scouter didn't seem suspicious. 'Yes, I can understand your asking. It would be helpful, wouldn't it, to know that the rest of us are safe from danger?'

'Yes, sir. I think it would.'

'Well, I can tell you that Mr Baynton was a

respected member of staff, and popular among the teams he managed. In fact, he was so successful here that he had begun refereeing for some local teams outside school as well.'

'You don't know if he had any enemies or anything . . .'

'Now, Daniel. I'm certain that the police are doing a very fine job of investigating Mr Baynton's sad demise. They will keep everyone safe – there's no need to worry. You should really try to put the whole thing out of your mind.'

There was a knock at the door. Mr Chayning opened it and poked his head in.

'Any chance of a chat, Mr Scouter?' he said. 'I'm on a free period and was hoping you could look at my proposals for saving the psychology GCSE course next year.' Mr Chayning's eyes were full of hope as he gazed through a pair of old-fashioned rimless specs.

'I'm terribly sorry, Mr Chayning, but these boys are my priority right now. They were the ones who found Mr Baynton yesterday.'

Mr Chayning's lip twitched at the name. 'I'm sorry to hear that. I'll just wait outside, then.'

'Yes, by all means, wait.' Mr Scouter turned back

to us as the door shut. 'I'm not sure how he got past Mrs Fustemann. Anyway, where were we? Oh, yes. Do you think it would be wise for me to arrange psychological support? You may have some lingering concerns,' Mr Scouter said, sliding forward in his chair.

'I think I'm all right, actually . . .' Daniel trailed off, not sounding nearly certain enough.

'Sir, we'll be fine. We can provide each other with peer support, can't we, Daniel?' I cut in, grinning in a responsible, stress-free way and jabbing Daniel's knee with mine.

'Oh – yes, of course, we can do that,' Daniel gabbled.

Mr Scouter looked unconvinced. 'As your headmaster, I have a duty of care to make sure this incident doesn't have long-term consequences on your young minds.'

My brain skidded through the options.

'How about, sir, if we come and see you in a couple of days? And you could check up on us then?' A polite smile was welded to my face.

'I – yes, perhaps that would be best. But please do feel free to pop in and speak to me if you need to, at any time. I will tell Mrs Fustemann that you are to

take priority over any standard school business.'
He looked at me with his wrinkly eyes all kind.
'This isn't the best start for you, is it, Jonathan? I
hope you won't judge the whole school on this one
dreadful tragedy.'

'No worries, sir,' I said. 'Our stay in Hanbridge
might be temporary, anyway.'

'Oh, I do hope not.' Mr Scouter shook his head.
'You'll soon settle in, and you're making friends
already, aren't you?'

Daniel stood up and I followed him, grabbing the
last fruit shortcake on the way.

'Thanks, Mr Scouter,' Daniel said, and Mr Scouter
leaped over and opened the door.

Mrs Fustemann gave us the evil eye for taking up
Mr Scouter's precious attention as she bustled
straight in with a pile of printed forms. The other
office staff all looked up from their screens and
stared at us again.

It was like being famous, but for all the wrong
reasons.

16

Wednesday 14 May, 12.40 p.m.

Hanbridge High School

Class was horrible. Everyone knew, obviously, that I'd seen Mr Baynton's dead body, and I heard a few of them laughing about it.

Tyler Jenkins was in this class, with his mate Jerome. Tyler gave me a long side-eye glance as I took my seat and, from the way Jerome was leaning forward at his desk behind me, I got the feeling trouble was coming my way.

'What did he look like, Inspector Clouseau?' Kelis Thompson[16] sat opposite me, and her grin

16 Kelis must have been watching old films – specifically, the *Pink Panther* series. Clouseau is like the anti-Sherlock, chaotic and bungling.

was wide, waiting for my answer. Tyler turned his chair towards me, and Jerome was now so close I could hear him popping his gum.

I did not want to get *that* as a nickname. I made a gruesome face at Kelis, but before I could tell her to shut up, Mr Peters interrupted.

'Now, Kelis, that's not a topic for discussion today. Boys, sit back properly, please. Jonathan has had a difficult experience and he is not here to satisfy your morbid curiosity. Frank, can you tell us something about the seven deadly sins?'

I got lucky. Mr Peters kept us busy for the rest of the lesson, but I could tell there were more questions bubbling up in most of the kids sitting around me.

At breaktime I hid in the library. There were a few good mysteries squirrelled away in the crime section but I didn't bother getting them out. I wouldn't have time to read them before I went back to Grensham.

Unfortunately there was nowhere to hide in the canteen at lunchtime. As soon as I walked in, all these heads turned to look at me. For the first time, people were patting seats next to them, keen to pump me for information. I queued up behind some fellow

---

Not a flattering comparison IMHO.

Year Sevens who were thankfully too shy to dare ask me anything. I tried to ignore their whispers, letting the noise of clanking serving spoons fill my head and the smell of minced beef fill my nose.

Plate of shepherd's pie on my tray, I finally looked around for somewhere to sit. Not to my left, cos there was Lydia Strong, staring at me with way too much interest. Right, there were Jerome and Tyler, eyes welded to my face. And there in the middle of the room sat Daniel, surrounded by Year Eight girls who showed no interest in him whatsoever.

There was no point playing it cool. That ship had already sailed.

I weaved around the tables and grabbed a seat opposite him. He was off in space, by the look of his glazed eyes and untouched food.

'Oi, Earth to Daniel. Come back to us.' I clicked my fingers under his nose.

'Oh, hi, Jonathan. Sorry, just thinking about how useful a replicator[17] would be in this canteen.' Daniel picked up his fork and poked gingerly at his jacket potato. 'I'm pretty sure these are not Heinz beans.' His eyes were still pinkish, like he'd hardly slept.

17 Futuristic food-producing miracle machines, apparently.

'*Heinz* beans? Do you think the school is made of money?' My pathetic non-joke actually made Daniel smile.

'How's your morning been?' he asked.

'Pants. Everyone wants to know what the corpse looked like.'

Daniel flinched. 'Yeah, same here.'

'How's your mum today?' I asked him.

'Didn't have the best night,' Daniel said quietly.

'Oh. That's bad, sorry. How about Mr Baynton's friend – Gavin, was it? Anything about him?'

Daniel shook his head. 'Nope. Mum might find out today, though.'

'You boys keeping these seats?' A voice behind me interrupted. It was Zaara, the girl from the office, with her tray of canteen food and a look of greedy interest that I was starting to get used to.

'Help yourself.' Daniel smiled. 'Everything going well with your apprenticeship?'

'Yeah, it's not bad apart from working for The Dragon. Better than a supermarket job. Anyway, you guys found Mr Baynton? That's put the cat among the pigeons.'

'How come?' Daniel asked her quickly, shooting a glance at me. I was low-key impressed – he'd twigged that she might be a good person to tell us stuff from the headmaster's office.

Zaara leaned forward in her seat and checked there wasn't anyone listening. 'Mr Baynton wasn't really the flavour of the month, here. Quite a few teachers couldn't stand him. Mr Chayning was mad because his GCSE was getting the axe, yet the PE department got new iPads to take the register on. Mr Baynton had been showing off about it, I think. And Mr Baynton's boss, Ms Zheng, said he was unprofessional because he spent most of his time on his phone, and "didn't give a damn about you kids" except the sports fanatics.' Zaara leaned back finally. 'Mrs Fustemann wasn't his biggest fan, either,' she finished, picking her fork up and stabbing at a piece of pie.

'Oh, really?' Daniel was interested. 'Did they not get on?' he asked.

'Well, strictly between us, I saw Mr Baynton having a bit of a row with Mrs Fustemann last week. He was going for a Head of House job, probably to annoy Ms Zheng cos she's Head of Carwood as well as Head of PE. And I know, we all did, that there were much better candidates, but he was being right cocky about it. I heard him – he reckoned the job was as good as his. The Dragon was livid, tried to shut him down, but he was right up in her face saying she didn't scare him, and he had a mind to report her . . .'

'Report her?' Daniel's expression was all intense. 'For what?'

'Dunno. She said he should "look to his own glasshouse before throwing stones", whatever that means.'

'But what's the story with him and Ms Zheng?' I dived in before Daniel could ask another pointless question. I mean, clearly the argument with Mrs Fustemann could be relevant, and maybe Mr Chayning might just be angry enough about iPads to commit murder, but Ms Zheng was a proper triathlete, and one of those teachers you definitely do NOT mess around. She had discipline and fair play written right through her. If Mr Baynton had managed to get under Ms Zheng's skin, who knows what might have happened?

'The Zheng thing? That started last year. They got really competitive over sports day – which house would win, you know? Carwood got the trophy. Ms Zheng rubbed his face in it, and after that it was like they just constantly wound each other up.' Zaara gulped down some water. 'They started doing nasty little pranks on each other, like, once he hid all the netballs just before an inter-school tournament she was organizing. And he supported Bristol Rovers, so one time Ms Zheng bought a massive Bristol *City* flag and hung it in the PE office. I heard her sniffing around the office a bit the other day, come to think of it, asking questions about refereeing he was doing outside school or something.'

Sounded like petty stuff, but probably worth looking into. I could imagine Ms Zheng's reaction to us sticking our noses into her business. It could only help Plan B if I got a bunch of detentions from her.

The room was starting to clear – the bell would ring before long.

'Right, boys! It's been a pleasure, but I've got to get back to my desk before one o'clock. Half an hour for lunch; they're taking the mickey.' She got up and took her tray over to the stacker by the hatch.

'We've got a starting point!' Daniel said once Zaara had gone, looking more cheerful than I'd seen him.

I shrugged like I didn't much care, when really my brain was whirring. 'We've got several possibilities.' I counted them off on my fingers. 'Mr Baynton's friend Gavin? We don't know what they were fighting about yet. Ms Zheng – seems unlikely on the face of it, but we can't rule her out, and they had a definite professional rivalry thing going on. Mr Baynton was picking on Mr Packington, and Mr Chayning was mad about his class getting cancelled and the money going to PE, so they've got motive but maybe not means. Mr Sinclair and Mrs Sudely could be minor suspects, but probably not the murderous types, and Mr Frantock was discussing alibis with Miss Black-Dudley, so that might be something. Then there's Mrs Fustemann – she has a temper but she's super respectable and has way too much to lose if she got caught. Mr Scouter and that office are her whole life. She adores him.'

Daniel looked at me frowning, probably in awe of my detective skills. 'Maybe – but what if Mr Baynton knew something that threatened her job? We ought to figure out where she was the night Mr Baynton died,' he said.

Hmm, I'd forgotten that bit. 'OK . . . but how are we going to do that? I'll just waltz up to her desk and ask, shall I?'

'I know how you can find out,' said a loud voice behind me.

Freaking Lydia.

17

Wednesday 14 May, 1.10 p.m.

Hanbridge High School

'What do *you* want?' I was rude, but that's the only thing that gets rid of stickybeaks like her. I glanced around, hoping no one was watching me talk to her. She was the least popular girl in our year, thanks to all her snooping around for stories, and another person I didn't want bullies like Tyler associating me with.

'I heard you. You're actually trying to figure out who killed Mr Baynton, aren't you? Why?'

'It's got nothing to do with you,' Daniel muttered.

'Yeah! Clear off,' I added.

'Will I hell! I want in.' Lydia crossed her arms.

'Why are *you* so interested?' Daniel's eyes had gone a bit glittery. Lydia's flaming-red hair contrasted with his washed-out locks.

'You losers won't get far on your own, will you? I'm good at this stuff. It's basic journalism. And there are some places I can go that you can't,' she said, chin in the air.

'Like where? And don't say the girls' toilets,' I replied, hating myself for getting sucked into her argument.

'Like, I can find out where Mrs Fustemann was the night before last. It's a matter of asking the right way, that's all.'

'She will bite your head right off and eat it,' Daniel said.

'Maybe. But if I do it, you have to let me join in with your detecting. Deal?' She put her hand out. I'm surprised she didn't spit on it first.

Daniel shook his head. 'No! It's not your business.'

'Just as much mine as yours.' Lydia smirked.

She was terrifying. Nosy, insensitive, and Daniel clearly didn't want her anywhere near his mum's secret – she'd probably make it a front-page splash. Problem was, she already knew too much to be let out of our sight.

Keep your friends close and your enemies closer.

I thought hard for a few seconds and then offered her a deal. 'How about – if you get *useful* information about Mrs F, you can help. OK?'

Lydia looked triumphant. 'Easy as pie. I'll meet you after school and tell you what she says. By the gates, yeah?' She grabbed Daniel's hand and shook it by force. I put mine in my pockets.

The bell went, and we heaved our bags on to our shoulders. Daniel gave me an eye-roll and I couldn't help grinning back.

That afternoon dragged. I kept quiet and avoided looking at anyone, in case they started asking about dead bodies again. I was starting to feel like a TV star in the supermarket queue – all eyes on me, expecting to be cornered and peppered with selfie requests. My mind kept straying to our list of suspects, particularly Ms Zheng. Being annoyed with someone wasn't the strongest grounds for murder (literally nothing compared to the motive Lois Baynton had), but we definitely needed to rule her out if we were going to do this properly. Plus, annoying an already irritated teacher was an easy way to keep Plan B moving along.

At 3.00 p.m. I put away my woodwork (a half-started bird box) and jogged out of the DT building through the yard to the front gate. Lydia was already there, looking well happy with herself.

'I've got news!' she yelled at me from twenty metres away.

'Shut up! We've got to be discreet.' I pulled her away from the stream of kids leaving school, half of them on their phones already and the rest talking and laughing. I remembered with a sharp pain what that was like, having mates to banter with.

'Hey! Don't push me around.' Lydia was glaring at me and patting down her uniform where I might have crumpled it up a bit. 'You don't want to get on the wrong side of me, Jonathan Archer. I've got martial-arts skills you could only dream of.'

'Sure, Lydia. What did you find out, then?' I asked, sensing she would go on for hours about herself given half a chance.

'Let's wait for Daniel.' She looked at me with a knowing grin. 'I know he must be driving this investigation of yours. You've only been here five minutes, you wouldn't know Mr Baynton from a hole in the ground.' She sat down on a bench.

I stood a bit further away, trying to make it clear to anyone watching that we had zero to do with each other. I looked at my phone – no messages – and wondered what the old crew were doing right now. Wednesdays were band rehearsal night. Maybe they were practising that Eagles song we'd been working on for ages.

Maybe they were auditioning for my replacement.

Daniel turned up a minute or two later.

'Come on,' I said as he crossed the grass. 'She says she's got something.'

'Sorry I'm late,' he said. 'Tyler wrote some rude stuff on my locker. Permanent marker. I was trying to get it off with hand sanitiser.' Daniel shrugged, like this was an everyday thing.

'What's he got against you?' I asked. Daniel was OK. He didn't need all this grief.

'No idea. Never liked me much, though. At least this time he didn't write NERD on my forehead.'

'Jonathan!'

What?

I had totally not believed my mum would come to meet me.

I ran to where she stood just inside the gates.

'What are you doing? We have been waiting outside.' Max was asleep in the pram.

'You actually came. Oh, *Mum* . . . do you have to show me up?'

'I told you, it is too dangerous for you to be walking home alone.'

'Gaaaahhh. Look, I just need a quick word with Daniel and Lydia. Can you wait out of sight somewhere?'

Mum looked over at them, then back at me. She smiled. 'You are making friends. Well done, Jonathan! Would you want to introduce me?'

Damn it. I didn't want her thinking I was building new friendships and settling in. But before I could say anything, she marched forward with her battering pram, all interested like this was a significant moment or something.

'Hello! I'm Jonathan's mother, Anneka. This is his brother Maximilian; he's asleep. Now, Jonathan, introduce your friends, please.'

I sighed but got on with it. If I refused, she'd only yell at me in public.

'This is Daniel and Lydia. They were just going to tell me about . . . a project we have to do for homework.' I shot the pair of them a look.

Lydia surprised me. Her face went all innocent and smiley, like she was channelling a CBeebies presenter. 'Nice to meet you, Mrs Archer. Jonathan is our buddy. Like, a new pupil gets a couple of buddies to help them through the first few weeks?' She shook Mum's hand and nudged Daniel to do the same. 'I was just going to suggest to Jonathan that he and Daniel pop over to my house to talk about maths. It's going to take a little while to explain to Jonathan what we've been doing in class before he joined, and we could have tea and biscuits, but if you need him to come home first . . .?'

I froze. Did I *want* to go to Lydia's house? About as much as I wanted an attack of the squits. Of course, the alternative was Daniel finding out what Lydia knew now, while I had to wait till tomorrow. I raised my eyebrows hopefully at Mum.

I could see that she was charmed; Lydia's manners were everything a parent could wish for.

'Well, no, I don't need him so desperately, it was just because of the . . . Yesterday's events were quite a horrible shock, and I was worried. Where do you live, Lydia?'

Lydia's bright smile went up a notch. 'I live on Rounceval Street, Mrs Archer. Not far from the shops.'

Mum nodded. 'Very well, Jonathan. Perhaps Daniel will be kind enough to walk back with you?

Make sure you're home by five at the latest, as I'll be putting tea on the table. And you should be doing some music practice when you get in, it is weeks since you played on your guitar! You will be losing proficiency.'

She pushed the pram in a tight turning circle and off she went. Daniel came out of his stress-daze long enough to notice that she was leaving and give her a Vulcan salute.[18]

'Maybe it's best if you leave the talking to me from now on?' Lydia snorted. She stomped off while I was trying to think of a good retort, and we ended up following her down the road like little lambs.

---

18 Spock's greeting in *Star Trek*. To give it, you raise a hand with your thumb extended while your fingers are parted between the middle and ring finger. Google it if you can't imagine what that looks like!

18

Wednesday 14 May, 3.25 p.m.

Lydia's house

We stopped outside a fiercely well-kept bungalow on Rounceval Street. The garden was laid out in strict rows of roses and leafy bushes, all trimmed to sharp, hard shapes.

'Right,' said Lydia as we went up the crazy paving behind her. 'This is where I live. It's my grandparents' house. Mind your manners, take your shoes off and don't mention murders. The codeword I shall use is MATHLETICS.'

She rang the doorbell.

A blurry shape came towards us behind the frosted glass. I tried to straighten my tie.

'Lydia! You didn't tell me that you were bringing home ... friends?' The last word was definitely a question.

Lydia's gran was not what I expected. She had blonde-grey hair all piled up in a complicated style and lots of lipstick. She wore bright-blue trousers, pointy slippers and a Greenpeace badge.

'Who are these two young gentlemen?' she asked.

Lydia had her angel mask on already. 'This is Daniel, from school – you remember, he was sick on the coach to Wales in Year Six? And this is Jonathan, who recently moved here from Oxford. We're all keen on maths so we're going to discuss setting up a mathletics club.' Her sweet smile wouldn't have fooled me for a minute, but Lydia clearly knew how to handle her gran.

'Then you'd better come in. Shoes off, please, I've just cleaned the floor. And don't forget, Lydia, it's taekwondo at six o'clock.'

The house was dark. All the furniture was old, and there were actual paintings hung on the walls. Lydia's gran showed us into the dining room off the hall. It had a light wooden floor and there were dried flowers in a vase on the table.

'I'll get you all some drinks. Please leave the door open.' She strode off down the corridor, her slippers tapping all the way to the kitchen.

'How come you live with your grandm...?' I started to ask. I realized it was a seriously personal question as I said it, and tried to swallow the words.

I tensed up, waiting for a Lydia eruption.

Lydia looked up coolly. 'Grandpa too, actually, but he's probably out at the allotment.' She nodded her head towards the hallway. 'They're my mum's parents. Mum and her partner live in Sri Lanka – they run a surf school. They're really busy, and I don't speak the language, so they left me here with Gran and Gramps.'

'Oh. OK. Is that ... Do you mind?' I asked, encouraged by her lack of rudeness.

'Do I mind? That's a bit of a stupid question, new boy. This town is really boring without her, but Mum wants to do the job she loves, so ... They come back in the holidays, sometimes.'

'I remember your mum. She had lots of piercings. She wore a Bajoran[19] earring once, like Kira in *Deep Space Nine*.' Daniel broke his silence. 'I didn't know

19 According to Daniel, Bajorans are humanoid aliens with wrinkly noses. Don't know why you'd want to dress like one.

she'd gone abroad, though.' He took the seat next to Lydia as we heard a tinkle from outside.

Gran came in with three glasses of squash and a small plate of Nice biscuits (not accurately named) on a wooden tray. She popped it on the table.

'Mind you use the coasters, please. Do sit down, er, Jonathan, was it? Lydia, get your elbows off the table. Now, if you're all set – *Gardener's Question Time* has just started on Radio Four . . .'

'Thanks, Gran, this is perfect. You go and listen to your programme.' Lydia did a big wide-eyed smile again as Gran exited the room.

'Right, let's talk about "Maths Club".' I tried to bring them both to the point quickly. I certainly wasn't there for fun. 'I've got to be home by five.'

'OK.' Lydia turned all businesslike. 'So, I went to the office after lunch because I knew Mrs Fustemann keeps a supply of sanitary towels . . .'

I put my fingers in my ears. Too much information.

Lydia folded her arms. 'If you can't cope with normal bodily functions you should not be investigating a murder.'

'Just ignore him. I don't mind. Go on, what did you say?' Daniel looked really interested so I took my fingers out and listened (although I still cringed a bit).

'I went in and asked if I could look through the lost property. I was kidding about my period. I just wanted to see your faces.'

Grrr. I had to remind myself there was a pressing reason to put up with Lydia. For now.

'Mrs Fustemann was her usual horrible self. I pretended I was feeling chatty while I went through the jumpers and made some small talk. You know she's got a *Corrie* calendar next to her desk? I asked her if she'd seen *Coronation Street* on Monday.'

We nodded impatiently.

'So she went, "No, I was taking notes at the governors' meeting", and I said did you watch it on Plus One then, and she was all, "No, I went to the cinema with my sister, I'll watch it on playback, now get on with looking for your jumper." Which means *obviously* she's a suspect – she wasn't back home till late.'

'Mr Scouter was on about a governors' meeting too. So she will have been at school until gone eight thirty, with, like, Mr S and the vicar. If she was at that meeting, and then with her sister, doesn't that give Mrs Fustemann an alibi?' I asked.

'We don't know if she has a sister, *or* if she even stayed at the meeting the whole time!' Lydia said triumphantly. 'We just know she wasn't at home watching her very favourite programme. There must have been a really good reason for that.'

I shook my head, which was swimming with info and suspects.

None of us had a clue what we were doing.

19

Wednesday 14 May, 3.55 p.m.

Lydia's house

Daniel saw my expression. 'We have to start somewhere, Jonathan. And we know a fair few things, so far.'

'That's true,' I said. 'OK. Have you got a piece of paper, Lydia?' We might as well try to use a bit of logic and order, like the cops on TV. It wasn't a murder board but it would have to do.

Lydia went to the sideboard and pulled out a notebook and pen.

I turned to an empty page. 'Let's make a list of who's who.' I wrote MR BAYNTON'S MURDER at the top.

'The first thing we know is that Mr B was killed – strangled – on Monday night. Most of the staff left by six p.m., but the governors were in school from seven p.m. until eight thirty p.m. plus a bit of chatting time.'

'Who are the governors? Maybe it was one of them,' Lydia said.

'They're, like, parents and businesspeople and pillars of the community,' Daniel said. 'Can't imagine they'd take that sort of risk?'

'Not unless it was a really *good* reason,' Lydia said. 'But we should check. Do either of you have any phone data so we can google it? Gran doesn't believe in Wi-Fi.'

I didn't, but Daniel had a few megabytes. His phone was incredibly slow.

'School website ... About us ... Our governors ... ooh, meeting minutes have been added already.' Daniel clicked a link. 'Say what you like about The Dragon, but she is efficient.'

'Does it say who was there?' I asked.

'Mr Martin, chair; Mrs Fustemann, secretary; Rev. Dawson, community representative; Miss Law, local authority; Carol Jones, parent governor; Ms Zheng, teacher governor; Mrs Scouter, financial adviser.' Daniel reeled them all off and I copied them down.

'Mrs F and Ms Zheng were there all evening.' I sighed. 'The rest of them sound so unlikely. I just can't see someone called Miss Law sneaking out of the back of the school to commit terrible crimes. But I guess we should keep a note of them all, in case none of the main suspects work out.'

'Surely we can narrow it down a bit? The police told us that the shed wasn't locked – so Mr Baynton either opened it himself or his killer had keys,' Daniel said.

He really was better at this than I thought he'd be.

'Which means the killer was someone he knew well, right?' Lydia leaped in, quick as a dart. 'Or someone with easy access to the school grounds.'

'I bet Mrs Fustemann has a pass to everything,' Daniel said.

So Ms Zheng had a senior teacher's pass, and Lois Baynton was seen at school, I thought. Based on her arrest, I was pretty confident that Lois Baynton was not Mrs Innocent, but there was no point saying this to either of these two. I didn't want our investigation to fizzle out before my parents had even found out about it.

'We shouldn't just focus on The Dragon, even if she is looking very suspicious,' I said. I thought about Mr Baynton's secret bank account and who might have been giving him those random sums of money – assuming his death was related to them. I wished I'd been the one who'd taken Mr B's notebook home with me, instead of Daniel. I was itching to try and untangle the mystery of those scribbled initials and numbers.

'Ms Zheng is all right, I swear.' Lydia shook her head. 'Yes, she's strict, and yes, she's stronger than Iron Man, but she's one of the goodies. Everyone likes her.'

'Everyone except Mr Baynton,' I said. 'We need to find out whether she left at the same time as all the other governors. I can do that, if you like?'

Lydia cackled a bit. 'Or *I* could talk to her in PE tomorrow. You're a newbie, Jonathan, she wouldn't tell you anything. I, on the other hand, am a top goal-scoring forward on her hockey team, so she knows me pretty well. And I have something of a reputation for curiosity around here already, being the school reporter and all. I might be able to ask Mr Chayning and Mr Packington more about their little feuds with Mr Baynton too.'

I nodded. Lydia was annoying, but she probably was better placed to grill Ms Zheng. Then I thought of something. 'Mr Baynton was holding that piece of newspaper in his hand when he died. That's a clue! Lydia, has your gran got this week's *Hanbridge Gazette*?'

'Probably. Hold on, I'll look in the recycling.'

We heard Lydia go into the kitchen where a loud posh voice on the radio was saying something about protecting hostas from slug invasion.

'Should we tell Lydia about going to the Bayntons' and the filing cabinet?' Daniel whispered.

'No way,' I muttered as she came back with the paper. I didn't want her patronizing us about what we'd done the previous evening.

'Can you remember which page was torn?' I asked Daniel.

'Let me have a look at it . . . Oh, this one. I remember the headline, about school fundraising. It's got a picture of some Year Eight students with Mrs Fustemann, Mr Scouter and the food tech teachers – they had a "back to school bake sale" last week . . .'

'So The Dragon is definitely implicated. Why else would her picture from the paper have been in Mr Baynton's hand?' Lydia said triumphantly.

'But there are other things here, like sports reports,' I said, turning over the page to examine the other side. There was an ad that caught my eye. It wasn't something I thought Daniel would like me to broadcast. I gave him a glance to see if he'd noticed it.

Daniel thought for a moment. 'So you're going to try and find out about Ms Zheng, Lydia, and I've got –' his face coloured up – 'questions to ask about someone we *haven't* listed.' He leaned over and wrote a new name in the suspects column.

Lydia was right on it, nostrils flared. 'Who's Gavin?'

Suspects	Timeline	Evidence
1. MRS FUSTEMANN: ROW	• Mr Baynton and Lois argue 5.30 pm	• Shed open
2. MS ZHENG: FEUD	• Mr Baynton back at school/other teachers leave by 6.00 pm	• Strangled by hand
3. MR PACKINGTON: BULLYING ETC		• Photo of Mrs Fustemann in local paper
• Too lazy to bother?		
4. MR CHAYNING: IPADS(!)	• Governors' meeting 7.00–8.30 pm	
• Unlikely!	• 9.00 pm + Mrs F at cinema with sister?	
5. MR FRANTOCK/ MISS BLACK-DUDLEY: MYSTERY RE. ALIBIS		
6. MRS SUDELY: DODGY CONVO WITH MR SINCLAIR		
7. GAVIN: FIGHT		

20

Wednesday 14 May, 4.20 p.m.

Lydia's house

Daniel tried to ignore her question. 'Jonathan, maybe you could look into Mrs F's alibi, or her motive?'

'Why have I got to do Mrs Fustemann? I've no clue how to get anything out of her.' I shivered as I remembered her beady eyes and the long red talons stabbing the air as she'd answered the phone. 'She is The Dragon, after all.'

'I'd say more of a Borg queen,'[20] said Daniel. 'And there's still other teachers to investigate. What did

---

20 The Borg are some of the scariest *Star Trek* aliens, and their Queen is the most intimidating of all. We watched an episode of *Voyager* with her in, and Daniel gulped like a goldfish when she came onscreen.

you hear about Mr Sinclair and Mrs Sudely, Lydia? They were talking outside the staffroom about Year Tens and safeguarding or something, but you said that was nothing to do with the crime.'

'Oh, yes! That was one of my scoops for the school paper last term – they refused to print it. Censorship, I call it. Erin Sommerville from form Ten E told me that Mr Sinclair and Mrs Sudely took them on a Duke of Edinburgh Silver trip, and several of them sneaked out of their tents after dark and had a party in the woods. The Year Tens, I mean. Like I said, it was hushed up. I expect the teachers were just nervous about it getting out, if the police went around asking the pupils a load of questions.' Lydia shrugged her shoulders. '*I* know a way we can find out more about Mrs Fustemann, though. We could have a go at her Facebook profile, see if she posted any pictures or checked in anywhere.'

'How do you mean?' Daniel was puzzled. 'You don't know her passwords.'

'Oh, I've done it before. It's easy, especially with old folks – they use real-world security information like their place of birth or their cat's name. I can work it out with a bit of trial and error, I expect.'

'OK. Let's do that in the library tomorrow. We haven't got much time now,' Daniel said.

'What's the rush, Daniel?' Lydia asked. 'You still haven't told me who Gavin is. And why exactly *are* you two investigating this anyway? You must have a reason.'

Daniel's mouth drooped and he glanced at me. I tried to sweep in and smooth away the question, feeling the urge to protect his secret. 'Just because we like a murder mystery. Plus it was us who found the body –'

'And we want to see justice done,' Daniel chimed in.

Lydia looked at us both sideways. 'Hmm, OK, I believe you. Not a lot, though.'

'So what's your reason, Lydia? Why are you sticking your nose in?' Attack is always the best form of defence.

'Well, I want to make editor, like I said. I'd be the youngest since 1996! And, you know. I heard you two talking and thought I could help . . .'

'Really? That's it?'

'Well. I get bored. You can imagine, can't you? I wished I'd found the body. But I didn't.'

Daniel sat up, suddenly remembering something.

'Oh, Rebecca Marley moved away, didn't she? She was your bestie for years –'

'Rebecca Marley has nothing to do with this. I hardly miss her at all, and I have lots of other friends.'

I looked at Lydia and saw an expression I recognized. An expression I had each time I checked my phone and there were no messages from the Grensham lot. 'Yeah, fair enough.'

'I reckon we could – we could be a team. Like Scooby Doo's gang!' Lydia suddenly looked a couple of years younger, her smile making the sharp lines of her face all soft.

Daniel put a hand on her shoulder. 'I think we'd be a *good* team,' he said. 'Like 'Hanbridge Mystery Incorporated'? Ooh, or better, we could be 'Kirk, Spock and McCoy', maybe?' He still hadn't told her the real reason he wanted to find the killer.

I wasn't so quick to reassure her.

I knew it was a brilliant plan and everything but two days ago I didn't know this pair, and now I was part of some cosy *team*, detecting a crime that was never any of my business, in a town that wasn't going to be home for much longer? OK, so I felt kind of sorry for Daniel – the situation with his mum was really hard. And Lydia knew how to get stuff done, and she seemed keen to help with the investigation. But what was the point in making friends when I wasn't going to be sticking around? And I really didn't want to end up playing Lewis to Lydia's Morse.

I cleared my throat and got my phone out, making a show of checking the time. Then I pushed my chair back.

'You leaving, Jonathan?' Lydia's green eyes didn't miss a thing.

'Yeah, Mum just messaged. Tea's nearly ready. I'd better be off. I'll catch up with you tomorrow, Daniel.'

'Don't worry, Jonathan. We'll do our best to struggle on without you.' Lydia smirked, downing the last of her squash.

21

Wednesday 14 May, 4.35 p.m.

Nanna Rosie's house

It's hard to make a dramatic exit when you've got to find your shoes and coat and then ask someone to unlock the front door for you. Daniel gave me his puppy look again and Lydia went all Triumphant Ice Queen on me. She probably thought that without me there she could pump Daniel for info. But I could tell Daniel was never going to spill anything to her about his mum's fear of social services. Maybe it was easier for him to tell that stuff to me because I was a stranger.

It took over five minutes to actually get out of the house and by that time my cheeks were flaming like a rash with embarrassment. On the walk home I checked the group chat again, asking 'anyone online?' I got nothing back except a GIF of a cat falling off a windowsill from Kinsey. Once I got in, Mum, of course, wanted to know all about my play date with my new little friends.

'So did you get it sorted out? Maths project, wasn't it?'

'Yeah,' I replied.

'Why don't you go upstairs and unpack your clothes properly?' Mum said, but I didn't. No point making more work for myself when I finally forced them to give in. Instead I sat on my bed with my headphones in, thinking about what I'd seen on the other side of that page in the *Hanbridge Gazette*. The same ad I'd seen in the Bayntons' kitchen.

Yoga with Lois!
Movement, deep relaxation and breathing.
Suitable for all ages and abilities.

I understood why Daniel had left Lois off the suspect list we'd made, and I felt kind of bad for him – his judgement was obviously being clouded by all that worry about his mum. But Lois definitely had the means, motive and opportunity. One of us had to remain logical.

I felt a bit better until the newspaper arrived on the doorstep with Lois Baynton's picture all over the front page.

Dad was drinking life-giving gulps of coffee and looking at it over his cornflakes. 'Looks like they caught the culprit, Jonathan! Did you hear anything more about that police statement, by the way?' he said.

'No, and there's no point now. They've got Mrs Baynton, haven't they?' As I spoke I felt a twinge of something run through me. I couldn't help wondering how Daniel and his mum were doing. It made my neck prickle to think of Ms Horsefell seeing her best friend's image like that.

I shook it off as best I could. I couldn't let gooey feelings get in the way of my game plan.

At school, my newfound fame had suddenly gone again. It wasn't as much of a relief as I'd expected, sitting in the maths lesson with no one to talk to as we did simultaneous equation practice. I was back to being the awkward new kid who no one gave a monkey's about.

Around me were little gangs of friends exchanging

gossip and jokes. None of it meant anything to me. Just noise distracting me from the brackets and numbers.

I was stuck brooding all morning, and although I ran through all the mystery book plots I could remember, I couldn't come up with a decent way to investigate Mrs Fustemann's movements. Nor had I heard anything from my Grensham mates. Not even a text message since the cat GIF yesterday. I was clearly out of sight, out of mind.

Fate leant a hand. At the end of science, Mr Frantock asked for a volunteer to take some paperwork over to the school office for him. My hand shot up faster than the speed of sound, which meant I collected a few dirty looks from the kids around me. No one likes a creep.

I walked to the office with Mr Frantock's handful of forms. It was morning break and the corridors were heaving with people and the sound of opening crisp packets.

Mrs Fustemann was at her desk, typing busily away on her keyboard next to the holy shrine of St Ken of Barlow[21]. Her beady eyes darted up at me as I stepped through the door.

21 Long-running *Coronation Street* character and a bit of a heartthrob for the older ladieez.

'Yes? What do you want?' she snapped, clearly never in a good mood.

'Mr F-Frantock told me to give you this . . .' I stammered.

'Hmmm, I see. Thank you, Jonathan.' Her tone was begrudging to say the least. 'You didn't want to see Mr Scouter as well, did you? He's had enough distractions this morning, since his dear wife came by with the annual audit reports.' Her comments ended with a snarl, and a heavy side order of *Don't you dare disturb him too*.

'No, no! I'm absolutely fine.' My nerves were failing me, to be honest. I looked around her desk, in a last-ditch attempt to discover something new. There wasn't much on there; everything was tidied into baskets and filing trays. But my eyes widened as I spotted a gleam of silver metal in among the pens and rulers.

Her eyes flickered to the same spot. 'Well? Off you go! Chop, chop.'

As I opened the office door I looked back. She had picked up the object and was dropping it into a drawer in her desk. This was more than I'd expected to discover.

Was that the sports whistle missing from Mr Baynton's neck?

Perhaps she was a prime suspect, after all.

***

I saw Lydia during the next lesson, English. I was bursting to tell Daniel first, of course, but I knew I'd enjoy dropping a few hints to her about what I'd seen.

She didn't meet my eye once, though. At the end of the longest lesson I'd ever sat through, as the class filed slowly out, she tried to corner Mrs Sudely for an interview. I hung back, packing my bag up slowly, keen to hear what she had to say.

'Miss, can I ask you a few questions about Mr Baynton? It's for my feature in this month's school paper, and I know you want to encourage us to be as probing as possible. I'm looking for opinions about what kind of person he was, and why he might have been –'

Before Mrs Sudely could respond – and she didn't look all that impressed with Lydia's request – there was a high, echoing scream from down the hall. It had a note of total horror – enough to tingle the back of my neck.

'Stay there,' Mrs Sudely said, barging past the last few stragglers out of the classroom. She ran, against all school rules, down the corridor.

I'm quick; I was right behind her and heard her gasp as she reached the top of the stairs.

I looked over the rail to see what she was looking at. Just outside the school office, on the hard floor, was Mrs Fustemann, papers scattered around and beneath her, lying at an odd angle at the bottom of the stairs.

22

Thursday 15 May, 11.40 a.m.

School corridor

Her eyes were closed and a purple mark bloomed across her forehead. She looked like a toy thrown down by a toddler in a tantrum.

Lydia caught up and saw the fallen Dragon. 'What the –'

Mrs Sudely walked carefully down the stairs and put her fingers to Mrs Fustemann's wrist for a pulse. I saw Mr Scouter push past his wife and Zaara Hussam, craning to see what was going on.

Mrs Sudely looked up while opening Mrs Fustemann's blouse at the neck. 'Someone call an ambulance. Now!'

We stood like ice sculptures, most of us. A girl from my tutor group, who seemed to have her head screwed on, scrabbled in her bag and pulled out her phone.

I couldn't take my eyes off Mrs Fustemann after that. It was like a horrible replay of finding Mr Baynton on Tuesday morning: the odd angles, the bruising, the feeling of helplessness. I couldn't understand what was going on. Teachers started coming out of the staffroom and it was like they were moving in slow motion. Lydia grabbed my arm, trying to talk to me, but I couldn't understand her. It was all a hum, a buzz, noises all around me but none making sense.

Another teacher joined Mrs Sudely at the bottom of the stairs and took charge of the growing crowd of extremely interested teenagers at the top.

'Off you go now, everyone off to your next lessons. There's nothing to see here,' said Mr Frantock, ushering us away with sweeping arm movements and a shake in his voice that he couldn't disguise.

'She's not dead, then?' Lydia blurted out.

Everything flooded into focus again around me.

'No. Now off to class, Lydia Strong!' Mr Frantock said.

'I'm on the school newspaper, sir. It's a legitimate enquiry. Our readers need to know what happened.'

'And that's *legitimately* not your business! Now off you go –'

Lydia changed tactic. 'I just need to get over to the office, sir, about the theatre trip next week. I'm late with my payment and permission slip – if I could just –'

'Next lesson!' he bellowed, shocking Lydia into stepping back.

It should have been me, pushing it with Mr Frantock. He was Deputy Head, and keener to give out detentions than a silver-back gorilla in a bad mood. But it seemed that being a badass and getting into trouble was slightly harder for me than I'd anticipated. The only way I was going to get back to Grensham was by getting even deeper into this investigation.

'OK, sir, sorry. Come on, Jonathan.' Lydia gave up and we walked away. She had her hand on my arm, I realized, and I moved away from her to break the physical contact.

'I've got history now. Bye,' I said as we reached the end of the corridor.

'No, you haven't,' Lydia said, grabbing my arm again and shoving me into the girls' toilets.

23

Thursday 15 May, 11.55 a.m.

Girls' toilets, Hanbridge High School

'What are you *doing*, Lydia? I can't be in here! I'll get beaten up if people find out I've been hanging out in the girls' loo.' I'd never been in there before. It smelled way better than the boys' toilets, and it looked like there was actual soap in the dispensers. I was relieved to see that we were alone and the cubicle doors were all on the green and open.

'Shut up, Jonathan. This is important. What if Mrs Fustemann was the next victim?' Lydia's eyes challenged mine.

'The *next* victim?' I felt slightly dizzy. 'Do you mean, like, a serial killer is bumping off all the teachers?'

Lydia shrugged. 'Maybe. Or maybe she knew something? Or saw something, here at the school on Monday night, before she went to the cinema?'

I frowned, thinking about that gleam of silver falling into Mrs Fustemann's desk drawer. Lydia was right, but I didn't feel like letting on that I agreed – she was too cocky as it was.

'Or – maybe she fell down the stairs by accident? She is nearly a hundred and forty years old, Lydia. Old people fall over all the time. That's why they make big red alarm buttons for them to wear round their necks.'

'Not all old people fall over,' Lydia snapped. I'd forgotten about her gran and gramps. 'She isn't that old anyway, not old enough to retire.'

I felt an extra flush of guilt, remembering Daniel's mum, and how difficult she found the stairs. 'You're right, you don't have to be old to fall.'

'So Mrs Fustemann is definitely a person of interest in this case. It's quite possible she's a second victim, which is why I was trying to check what her movements were this morning and who was around at the time. Unfortunately, Mr Frantock wasn't having it.'

Damn. Lydia did, actually, make a good point – if

this was a crime rather than an accident, that meant Daniel could even be right about Lois being innocent, despite all the evidence against her. And it completely ruled out Mrs Sudely, as she was with us when Mrs F fell. But I still couldn't bring myself to admit Lydia was right.

'No way,' I said. 'I reckon she just slipped.'

'Look me in the eye and tell me you're sure it's an accident,' Lydia hissed, crossing her arms and getting right into my face so her freckles were only centimetres away. 'What if there's a murderer on the loose – I mean, there's no way Mrs Baynton is guilty of *this*, is there? She's locked up at the police station! So that means he, or she, has tried to kill again. If you don't want to do it for Daniel, do it to make sure no one else gets hurt.'

'What do you mean, do it for Daniel?' I pulled my collar away from my neck. I'm not sure why I was still trying to protect Daniel's secret, but it was like an automatic reaction. He'd made me swear not to tell a living soul, after all.

'I'm not stupid, Jonathan. I can tell when someone's not telling the whole truth. He clearly has a reason for wanting to find out who the killer is. And I thought that maybe you were trying to help him. Yesterday you even had lunch with him – no one's done that since Year Five! Then last evening at mine you started being all weird about it.' Lydia was still right up in my grill, making me feel all sweaty and under pressure.

I shrugged. 'I do want to help Daniel. It's just – I'm not here forever, you know. Only until my idiot parents sort themselves out. I've already *got* friends, good ones, back in Grensham . . .'

Lydia sniffed. 'Well, perhaps you'd better go and hang out with your long-distance pals, then. Me and Daniel can handle this without you.' She stomped off, shaking her bright-red plaits.

She almost got to the door before I cracked. After all, getting into trouble was the best and only plan I had.

'OK! OK. I'll help you. But . . . don't expect me to be your assistant, Lydia Strong. I'm not stupid, you know.'

'None of us are stupid. That's why we're going to make an amazing team,' Lydia said as she turned back towards me. 'We've got PE with Ms Zheng this afternoon. I can ask her about her movements on Monday. Then we'll all meet in the library at three fifteen – you two can watch my back while I try to hack into some social media accounts,' she concluded with a grin.

I nodded. 'Sounds like a plan. I'll text my mum and let her know I'll be late again – Mathletics is on.'

24

Thursday 15 May, 1.15 p.m.

Hanbridge High School

I decided to text Mum before I went to history, which was a seriously bad idea. Some girl from Year Eleven walked into the toilets and screamed when she saw me standing by the sink.

'Get out! This is a private space – get out, get out!' She flapped violently at me until I backed away into the corridor. Great. That was going to be yet another awesome addition to my cool reputation.

I was feeling pretty glum again by lunchtime. I knew it was going to be interesting, the whole murder investigation and everything, but it sucked watching the other kids bolt down their lunch to go and play ball, while I sat on my own eating soggy chips.

So I went and hid behind the science block and rang Jayden's number. He answered after like nine rings, laughing so hard I thought there was a bad line.

'Morticia! How's it going?'

'Hey! Yeah, all good. Can you call me back? Got zero credit.'

'Sure, sure, sure, speak shortly . . .'

The phone went dead. My grin was huge; it was so good to hear those tones again. Then it rang and I picked up quick.

'Hey, so how's everything in Pirate Land?' They'd all been joking about how I was going to end up with a Bristol accent.

'All right. No one even shoots hoops, though. I don't know what I've got to do to get a game going round here, seriously. It's proper quiet, apart from the murder . . .'

'Wow, yeah, I saw that on the news. Insane times.'

'Yeah, it was pretty full on, finding the dead bo–'

'Anyway, we're out playing five-a-side, everyone's here – hey, you lot, give Jonno a shout!'

I heard a chorus of 'oi, oi' and 'hey' and half a dozen other random greetings.

'Who's there?' I asked.

'Ah, the usual gang. Kinsey, Ant, Elliot, Georgia – oh yeah, and there's a new kid who started right after you took off. Desmond, such a funny guy, shame you can't hang out.' Jayden started laughing. I think his socks fell off, it went on so long. 'He's got this thing, right, where he nods slowly at Mr Sloth[22] when he asks him for answers and he's, like, totally no idea what to say to him.'

My chest suddenly felt a bit tight. 'Oh so, like, he's settling in well and that –'

'For sure! Plays a mean guitar too, actually. You'd like him. Look, I've got to go now – my turn in goal. Stay chill, yeah?'

The call ended. And just like that I was back on my own, hiding behind the science block, the warm feeling I'd got hearing my old friends' voices in the background of the call fading away.

Back to reality. I went and watched some kids playing netball while I waited for lunchtime to get over itself. This place *sucked*, and more and more

_____

22 His real name is actually Mr Gough, but he speaks so slowly everyone calls him Sloth.

I was realizing that Plan B to get out of Hanbridge wasn't working.

PE was straight after lunch. I was starting to take my tie off when Daniel put his star-spattered PE bag down next to my plain black one in the changing room.

'I heard you were there when Mrs Fustemann fell . . . I'm sorry you had to see it.' He turned his deep-brown eyes on me. 'Thanks for working on the plan with Lydia. I know she's not an easy teammate.'

I wished those two wouldn't keep going on about this team, like we owed each other allegiance or something. I was only helping out, and mainly helping myself.

'Did you hear Mrs F is in hospital? Head injuries and a broken arm.' Daniel's voice cut through the chatter again.

'That figures,' I said, thinking about the angle of Mrs Fustemann's body at the bottom of the stairs. 'At least she's alive.' Despite reading all those funeral books I'd nicked from Dad, the sight of one real dead body was more than enough for me.

I took the opportunity to fill Daniel in on the whistle I saw Mrs Fustemann trying to hide. 'I can't be sure it's Mr Baynton's, obvs, but it definitely looked dodgy. Do you remember – he wasn't wearing it when we . . . found him.'

Daniel's eyes sparked up. 'That's a great lead! At the very least she must know something, surely?'

'Yeah, but now she's out of our reach in hospital we might never find out what she was doing with it. And if it's not his, then it's a total red herring.'[23]

'Still. I feel like we're making progress. We can talk about it more after school.'

'Right, everyone,' Ms Zheng boomed into the changing room. She soon had us all lined up outside. 'Today we will be playing tag rugby, mixed teams. Let's sort you into groups of seven . . .'

Ms Zheng was not particularly tall, but she was stocky. Maybe in her mid-thirties. Eyes in the back of her head and sharp as flint, fully capable of sending a whole class to detention. But she was also fun, and fair. Lydia was right; she was intimidating but people respected her, even quite liked her.

Daniel got sorted into a different group but Lydia ended up playing against me on the opposite team.

23 Red herrings are the rotten clues that send you down the wrong path in a detective novel, by misdirecting or distracting your attention with their stink.

As captain, naturally. She was quick and ruthless and they won easily, partly thanks to her ability to slip through non-existent gaps between our players. Ms Zheng gave her lots of encouragement – 'Well done Lydia!', 'Great pass!' – so I guess she was right about being the best person to do the questioning. I wasn't sure when she was going to get a chance, though. Ms Zheng wasn't one for rest breaks.

At the end of the lesson, I saw Lydia fall in beside Ms Zheng as we walked back to the changing rooms. I hung back behind them to try and hear what they said.

'Miss,' Lydia started. 'Have you had to give any evidence? You know, about Mr Baynton's tragic death. Because you were in school all that evening, weren't you?'

Ms Zheng stopped suddenly, and I nearly trod on her heel.

'Why on earth do you want to know about that?' she asked.

I crouched down and very slowly tied an imaginary loose shoelace.

'You may not know this, Ms Zheng, but I am aiming for a career in journalism. So I'm trying to take every opportunity to hone my craft, interviewing people for practice. I'm writing an article about the events of this week and I need a range of bystander accounts.'

Ms Zheng pondered that bare-faced lie for a second. 'Lydia,' she said. 'Are you trying to be funny?'

'No, of course not! I'm merely gaining experience and conducting the kind of research that every young reporter needs under their belt.'

I squinted up and saw Lydia pulling her angel face, looking innocently into Ms Zheng's eyes. I moved to the other shoe.

Ms Zheng broke first. 'If it were anyone else, I would send you off with a flea in your ear. But I know things haven't always been particularly easy for you, Lydia. I also think you do in fact have a lot of the qualities suitable for journalism and combined with your abilities on the hockey field, you could even be the next Alex Scott or Gabby Logan. So I'm going to give you the benefit of the doubt this *one* time. I'm going to let you ask me three questions, only three, about Monday night. If I don't like your question, I won't answer it. Got it?'

'Yes, miss. Got it.'

Lydia and Ms Zheng started moving again, and

I cautiously followed them. I didn't want to miss any of this.

'So have you spoken to the police?' Lydia asked.

'As it happens, yes, I did have a chat with DI Meek. There was a lot to talk about with regard to Mr Baynton. That's your first question.'

Lydia waited in vain for more details. 'No fair, miss! That wasn't a real answer!'

'Take it or leave it, Lydia. What's next?'

Lydia frowned, deep in thought. I could almost hear the cogs whirring in her brain as she tried to think of a foolproof question. There was so much we didn't know – like why Ms Zheng was so interested in Mr Baynton's referee work outside school?

'OK. Who saw you leave the school after the governors' meeting?'

Ms Zheng squared her shoulders. 'Well, I suppose that's no secret. We all left together. Mrs Fustemann used her pass to let us out and then she held the gate for Mr Scouter and Reverend Dawson, who were lagging behind while Mr Scouter locked up. I was chatting with Harriet Jones's mum Carol about Harriet's ankle injury until I got to my car, so I guess she's my alibi. If that's what you're looking for?'

'Yes . . . I mean, thanks, miss. And you didn't see

anyth– NO, I take that back. That wasn't a question cos I didn't finish it.'

Lydia's forehead scrunched up as her brain went into overdrive. I was low-key worried that we were going to get back to the changing rooms before she'd had time to ask her last question. Then suddenly I had a flash of inspiration.

'What were you doing *before* the governors' meeting, miss?' I blurted out. They both swivelled around.

'Jonathan!' Lydia shot me a glance of pure outrage and then gazed appealingly up at Ms Zheng's wooden expression. 'That wasn't a question, either. I mean, it wasn't an official school newspaper question.'

'Nevertheless,' said Ms Zheng. 'I think that's probably enough for today. I decline to answer, Jonathan, and I'd better check that the girls are actually having showers and not just spraying themselves with extra body mist to hide the stink.' She strode ahead of us back towards the changing rooms.

'You *idiot*. I was THIS close to getting the info we needed out of her!' Lydia flounced off behind Ms Zheng and left me to head back into the boys' changing room, trying to convince myself it was ace that I'd finally got on the wrong side of a teacher.

25

Thursday 15 May, 3.10 p.m.

Hanbridge High School

Geography, last period. We had to colour in a map of Spain to show average annual rainfall. Massive yawnathon.

My heart gave a little skip when I set out to the library. I knew Lydia was going to give me a hard time, but it was still good to be making progress. Plan B was definitely the way to go. Plus, I'd remembered that Mum would be too busy feeding the Weetabix monster to supervise my walk home.

Lydia was already there, logging into the dusty old PC furthest away from the librarian's desk, too focused on typing to notice my entrance.

'Hey, Lydia. What'cha doing?'

Lydia glared over the top of the monitor. 'I'm using a proxy account to log into the school system without making it blindingly obvious that it's me. More importantly, what were *you* doing butting into my conversation with Ms Zheng earlier? You blew the whole thing!'

'I know, but if Mrs Fustemann was a second victim, then the culprit must have been someone in school, like a teacher or one of the office staff. All the governors will have been together during the meeting and they left together afterwards, so they all give each other alibis. So . . . maybe the murder was done *before* the meeting?'

Lydia looked at me and grunted. 'Huh. It's possible you're not completely wrong.' She went back to her keyboard and began typing again. She pointed to the seat next to her. 'Daniel will be here in a second.'

As she spoke, Daniel pushed through the double doors, his sandy hair flopping over his eyes and his backpack swinging. He knocked a couple of paperbacks off one of those twirly display stands and went red, stooping to pick them up while the librarian looked at him fondly.

'I've got those books here you reserved, Daniel – the Philip K. Dick and the Ursula Le Guin?' Miss Culham held out two chunky books.

'Brilliant!' Daniel scrabbled in his backpack for his library card. 'Any progress on that *Voyager* book you said you might order?'

Miss Culham smiled. 'I can't afford it new, but I'm doing my best on eBay. Never fear, I'll get hold of a copy!'

'Thanks, Miss!' Daniel replied, as he made his way over to us without any more accidents, and dropped his bag under the desk.

Lydia was typing hard and fast, keys clacking like gunfire. 'Hey, Daniel. You and Jonathan need to keep your eyes open for teachers. I'm going to be busy.'

I couldn't think of anything useful to say, so I looked around at the shelves. The library was a big, bright room plastered with posters, huge cut-outs of *Harry Potter*, that girl from *The Hunger Games*, and multicoloured paperbacks all stacked on high shelves. If I was sticking around, I'd be all over the murder-mystery section like a rash.

When I looked back, Daniel had dug a pair of handcuffs out of his bag.

'What the hell?' I pushed my chair a little bit further away. 'Do I want to know?'

Daniel looked not-embarrassed-enough. 'Oh, I keep them with me to practise. I'm learning escapology from this book. Look.'

He dived into his backpack and pulled out *Paul Daniels' Greatest Tricks*.

'Who on earth is Paul Daniels?'

'He was a brilliant TV magician in the eighties and nineties!' Daniel started clicking the handcuffs on his wrists in a professional manner. 'Look, see? There's a skill to it. He gives step-by-step instructions in the book.'

He did something complicated with his fingers and two seconds later the cuffs landed on the floor with a noisy jingle.

'*Shh*,' I said, looking up at the issue desk. Miss Culham had glanced in our direction.

We ducked out of our chairs and crowded around the back of Lydia's.

'OK. So, who shall we look up first?' She already had tabs open with Facebook, Twitter and Instagram.

I had a thought. 'Shall we start with Mr Baynton? As he's the only definite victim? He might have private messages or something.'

Lydia grinned at me. 'Right! We need his username. It said in the paper he was called Oliver . . .'

'He normally shortened it to Ollie,' Daniel blurted out.

Lydia spun round and looked at Daniel. He stared at the floor.

'And you know this because . . . of the reason you're investigating? The thing I don't know and you two do?' Lydia's voice was cross and fierce.

I stayed solid. Daniel crumbled slightly, but he knew better than to tell a reporter his secret.

'I'm really sorry, Lydia,' he murmured helplessly, giving her his puppy-dog impression. Lydia snorted.

'You can get around many people with that act, Daniel, but not me. I invented that act.' She turned back to the screen. 'So if you know his nickname, maybe you know his personal email address too? That'd be useful.'

Daniel shook his head.

'OK, we'll have a go with what we have got.'

I felt about as useful as the giant cardboard cut-out of Hagrid in the corner. I leaned on the back of Lydia's chair and turned my head to check that Miss Culham was busy at her desk. She was cutting out big laminated letters, so I figured we were safe for a bit.

'OK, so, Ollie Baynton at generic email account dot com. Now, password. Did you know that seventy per cent of all passwords are "password"?' She tapped it in and pressed enter. 'No. Password123? No. He wasn't a complete idiot, then.'

She glanced up at each of us in turn. 'OK, I'm going to have to try something a bit more heavyweight before it locks me out.' She gestured to the USB drive she had stuck in the port. 'I'm using this little beauty to bypass school security restrictions, and I'm going to run a hybrid dictionary attack, which will capture most of the alphanumeric options by blasting through every word from A to Z and all the combos in between. While that's running, we can log into another computer and check out Twitter, maybe. Daniel, you get started while I set this going.'

I was seriously impressed with Lydia's hacking skills, though I wasn't going to tell her that. Within a few minutes we were scrolling through Twitter on Daniel's computer while Lydia's screen flickered and buzzed with activity.

'The school has loads of different Twitter accounts – there's one for Art, another for English, and, aha – yep, there's Ms Zheng's PE account.' She pointed to the screen and Daniel dutifully clicked on the link to @HbridgeHighPE.

'So she tweeted today about deadlines for netball try-outs. Yesterday there was a reminder about not bringing nut products into school. Scroll down? She *did* tweet on the day of the murder, look, but it's just photos of trampolining club.'

Daniel leaned into the monitor. 'What time did she post these photos?' he asked.

'6.17 p.m. Trampolining club is on till 5.30, I think.'

'That's interesting,' I said. 'We heard from Lo– a *reliable source* that Mr Baynton was at home at 5.30 p.m., and the papers say Mrs Baynton followed him to school to continue an argument they'd been having. She got turned back by Mrs Fustemann between 5.45 and 6 p.m.'

Lydia raised an eyebrow. 'A reliable source, eh? So, the window of opportunity must be six to seven o'clock, between the school being empty of teaching staff and the start of the governors' meeting. But if Ms Zheng was tweeting right in the middle of that window – see, she answered several comments, posted soon after – it doesn't give her much of a chance to kill Mr Baynton.'

'I'm not sure she's a very good suspect, anyway,' Daniel said. 'She was probably doing paperwork or planning lessons.'

'She was a bit cagey earlier, though, when we grilled her after PE. We shouldn't rule her out completely,' I said. Without Ms Zheng, we were right back to square one and how guilty Lois was looking. After all, Mrs Fustemann might have fallen by accident, even though with the whistle it seemed like she had something to hide. 'She was definitely holding back info about Mr Baynton . . .'

'I just can't see how she'd manage to commit a murder while simultaneously keeping up with her social media accounts.' Daniel sounded resigned to losing another suspect.

'What about the other staff who hated Mr Baynton? He wasn't exactly Mr Popular,' I said.

'Well, we've ruled out Mrs Sudely now, as she was with us when Mrs Fustemann fell and that secret conversation with Mr Sinclair was just about the Duke of Edinburgh trip,' Lydia said. 'Then there's Mr Packington, Mr Chayning, Miss Black-Dudley and Mr Frantock.'

'I think Mr Packington is too lazy to commit murder,' Daniel said. 'He doesn't even get off his chair to hand the books round in maths – last week he just tossed them at us from across the room.'

'So should we update our list?' I said, pulling the crumpled paper out of my coat pocket.

Suspects	Timeline	Evidence
1. MRS FUSTEMANN: ROW	• Mr Baynton and Lois argue 5.30 pm	• Shed open
• Second victim??	• Mr Baynton back at school/other teachers leave by 6.00 pm	• Strangled by hand
2. MS ZHENG: FEUD		• Photo of Mrs Fustemann in local paper
• Alibi – Social media?	• Ms Zheng tweeting at 6.17–6.25 pm	• Second murder attempt on Mrs F?
• Cagey about time of crime	• Governors' meeting 7.00–8.30 pm	
3. MR PACKINGTON: BULLYING ETC	• School locked by 9.00 pm	
• Too lazy to bother?	• 9.00 pm + Mrs F at cinema with sister?	
4. MR CHAYNING: IPADS(!)		
• Unlikely!		
5. MR FRANTOCK/MISS BLACK-DUDLEY: MYSTERY RE. ALIBIS		
6. MRS SUDELY: DODGY CONVO WITH MR SINCLAIR		
• Alibi for Mrs F's accident/D of E cover-up		
7. GAVIN: FIGHT		

'The library is shutting in five minutes,' Miss Culham called across the room as she put away her scissors and tidied up the issue desk.

Lydia took a quick look at her hack-in-progress. 'Argh. No luck,' she said as she scanned through the gobbledygook on-screen. 'It hasn't had enough time to find the password.'

The three of us looked at each other. I heard my phone beep but this was no time to check my messages.

'We can't just give up,' Daniel said, twiddling with his handcuffs. 'Persistence *isn't* futile.'[24]

'But we're not going to get any further here. I do have another idea, though it depends whether the police have taken the IT equipment out of Mr Baynton's office.' Lydia stood up, removed her USB stick and flicked the power switch behind the PC. 'Follow me.'

24 *Star Trek* alien reference: 'We Are the Borg. You Will Be Assimilated. Resistance is Futile' is their standard line, on repeat. It's a great thing to say when Mum and Dad try and tell me what to do.

Thursday 15 May, 3.30 p.m.

Hanbridge High School PE office

We trooped out of the library and back through the corridors towards the PE department.

Just as we passed the science office, the door opened. Lydia grabbed us both and pushed us behind a tall storage locker. 'Look!' she whispered sharply in my ear.

Mr Frantock and Miss Black-Dudley came out together.

'We are doing OK, aren't we, Mark?' Miss Black-Dudley sighed, looking up into Mr Frantock's stern face.

He stopped, and we heard the sound of a squelchy kiss. *Noooooo. Cringe.*

'We are doing just fine, my love. No one suspects a thing.'

'That's good. But when *are* you going to call it off with your fiancée? You keep saying soon, but it's been months now. I just want to tell the world that we're together.' Miss Black-Dudley's voice was a little whiny, to be honest, and Mr Frantock's reply was about as kind as I'd expect from him.

'You must be patient, Helen. Now, we can't be seen together like this.' He stepped away from her. 'Back on professional terms, Miss Black-Dudley.'

Miss Black-Dudley sighed again, and they carried on walking along the corridor away from us. *Phew.*

'Well, that's them out of the running,' I said. 'The "alibi" they were whispering about the other day has nothing to do with Mr Baynton, does it?'

'Guess not. They were never my top picks, anyway.' Lydia shooed us along the way we were heading. 'Come on, let's go.'

Lydia stopped outside the PE office and shook the handle of the battered grey door. It was locked. There was a laminated notice tacked up, which said: '*Unless you have a signed note from a parent or guardian, you* will *be doing PE.'* Underneath, someone had scrawled in blue marker '*in your vest and pants if necessary'*. PE teachers are brutal.

Through the narrow window of the office we saw bits of desks. The nearest had a bunch of paperwork piled up along with whistles and sports bottles, and scrunched-up tabards were draped over the back of the chair.

'Mr B's desk is in the far corner,' Lydia pointed out. She rattled the door handle again. 'Big pain that we can't get to it.'

'I can unlock the door,' Daniel said, looking a bit flushed. He groped in his backpack and pulled out a skinny roll of cloth. 'These are my lock picks. Paul Daniels says they're essential to escape from locked boxes and wardrobes, so I ordered them on eBay.' He unrolled the cloth to reveal a row of thin metal tools. He went over to the door and probed in the keyhole with one of them.

I tried not to feel surprised. This was a very Daniel skill to have, after all. I stood behind him and kept an eye out for passing teachers. It occurred to me that getting caught in the act of breaking and entering might be a good move for Plan B. A good, scary move.

Twenty seconds later there was a big, fat click.

'There you go,' Daniel said, half embarrassed and half proud, pushing the door wide for us.

'Oh,' Lydia said.

There were three desks in the room. Mr Baynton's was cordoned off with police tape and with a layer of silvery dust over everything.

'They've been checking for prints.'

'Yes, Jonathan, obviously,' Lydia said. 'What are we going to do now?'

'Well – if they've dusted for fingerprints already –' Daniel looked sideways at me and Lydia – 'they might not notice if we have a quick look.'

'You mean ignore the police tape? That is *not* what I expected to hear from you, Daniel!' Lydia goggled.

Daniel shrugged. 'I guess it's like the Prime Directive of non-interference.[25] You're not supposed to ever break it, but half the time it's unavoidable, because of the needs of the many outweighing the needs of the few.'

'OK ... I take it that's a *Star Trek* reference. Completely baffling as usual,' Lydia said.

25 Basic rule of Starfleet: no crew member should interfere with the natural development of a primitive civilization.

'I just think we'll have to look at his computer if we're going to get anywhere.' Daniel was unwavering on this point.

Lydia's eyes turned and challenged mine. 'What do *you* think, new boy?'

I was less surprised about Daniel's attitude, after our little breaking-and-entering adventure on Tuesday evening. He had good reason for wanting to crack this case. His mum's peace of mind – actually, her whole health and family – were at stake. But I didn't leap on to the idea straight away. 'It's a bit risky.'

Was I *really* going to hesitate? Did I actually want to get in deep doo-doo, or didn't I?

'They must be finished with it, Jonathan,' Daniel said. 'Otherwise they wouldn't have left the computer here in the first place.'

'I reckon if Daniel's up for this, we all should be. Come on!' Lydia grabbed the blue and white tape and eased it out of the way.

I swallowed hard. Brilliant.

Lydia twisted herself into Mr Baynton's ergonomic chair and leaned over his keyboard (one with multicoloured backlights. Fancy.). 'Now, will Mr B have left us a handy Post-it . . .'

'What are you looking for?' I asked.

Daniel pointed to a note attached to the bottom of the screen. 'Password,' he squeaked. 'You're not supposed to leave it lying around, but loads of people do.'

The password turned out to be *BayntonWins100*. We logged on and opened a browser window, Lydia typing *facebo* into the address bar.

'Let's just hope . . .' Lydia breathed as she pressed enter.

The web address autocompleted and Mr Baynton's Facebook page loaded.

'He ticked the *remember me* box. Awesome.'

I glanced out of the window in the door for a few seconds, my mind lingering on the crime-scene tape.

'Let's get a move on,' I said. 'What's on his timeline?'

'Yeah, yeah, give me a couple of minutes.' Lydia was busy scrolling down the screen, past memorial posts ('Ollie, you will always be in our hearts'), then pictures of beer glasses and huge fried breakfasts. He had updated his page a lot.

Daniel leaned in and tapped the screen. 'We should be systematic about this. Let's see who he's in contact with.'

Lydia clicked on the *Friends* button.

'Are we going to type in names, or just browse the whole lot? He's got over six hundred people on here.'

'Browse,' Daniel said, already scanning the screen, which was covered with tiny thumbnails.

'OK, well, there's his wife.' I pointed at the top picture. 'And that's Mrs Sudely. I bet half the teachers are on here. He could have been killed by any one of them.'

'Yeah. Look – Mr Scouter, Mrs Scouter, Mr Frantock, Mr Packington, Mr Sinclair – ooh! Mrs Fustemann – our second victim!'

'Click on *view friendship*,' Daniel said, much bossier than usual. We waited for the page to load. 'Rats.'

There were no posts. No evidence of any contact between the two. No obvious reason why they should both be attacked.

A large shape passed the window in the door. I saw the back of a jacket as one of the DT teachers walked along the corridor outside.

'Guys. Come on,' I couldn't help mumbling, as my heart leaped sideways. I was annoying myself. Getting caught was the STRATEGY.

'What about messages?' Lydia clicked her fingers and then the icon. 'That's more like it.'

We quickly scanned through the names in the inbox.

'Ms Zheng!' Lydia blurted out, under her breath. 'Let's see – *Oliver, I know exactly what you've been up to out at BTHC and I am willing to take my information to the authorities. I hope you'll do the right thing and withdraw your application from the Head of House job, before I have to make you.*'

'Wow! Well, that's not what I'd expect from Ms Zheng. She really did hate his guts.' I whistled quietly. 'What do you think BTHC means? What was he doing?'

'Let's google it.' Lydia opened a new tab and typed in the initials.

What came up was less than helpful:

- The Buddhist Tai Hung College, offering an excellent English language education in Hong Kong.
- A Facebook page for Bad Taste House Collective in Brisbane, Australia (dodgy dance music).
- The Bentwood Trails Health Centre in Ontario, Canada ('We strive to help bring healing').

The initials had tugged on something in my brain. BTHC . . . where had I seen it before? I couldn't for the moment think what it was. We didn't even bother clicking on to the second page of results.

Daniel sighed. 'Not something obvious then. But surely Ms Zheng is back in the frame now?'

'Maybe. Are there other messages?' Lydia scrolled up. There was nothing else from Ms Zheng – and no reply from Mr Baynton. 'Let's see what else there is.' Lydia went back to Mr Baynton's Messenger account.

'Who's that?' Daniel leaned in again as Lydia clicked on a photo of a big, burly man.

'*Olley*,' it read. '*I need that money back, pronto. Drop it in at the shop tomorrrow or you know what'll happn. Stop messin me about.*'

'Who's Stan Waldron?' I asked.

Lydia clicked on his photo to get to his profile. He was listed as a 'local business entrepreneur', and his photos were ninety-nine per cent muscle shots. Arms, covered in tattoos, all clenched up to look massive and powerful.

'He looks scary,' I said, focusing on a shot of Stan Waldron baring his teeth like a tiger. I wrote his name on the suspect list in capital letters.

'Let's look at his "About" page, see where he's based – we could go and question him if it's nearby,' Daniel said.

I glanced at Daniel in surprise. That sounded like a terrible idea to me. I went and looked out into the corridor again. I couldn't seem to stop doing it.

'He's got a Cash4Cheques shop on the high street,' Lydia said. 'Hey – he's in a couple of groups – Friends of the School is one! Maybe he's connected to Mrs Fustemann . . . No, they're not friends. But they are both fans of local sports teams – Bristol City, Bristol Hockey and Hanbridge Town football team.'

'Why is that interesting? Come on, we should go now. We've got a lead, maybe two,' I said.

'Let me have one more peek at those messages . . .'

I looked out of the narrow window again. Straight into the face of DS Norman.

27

Thursday 15 May, 3.45 p.m.

Hanbridge High School

'Gah!' I dodged back from the door, but DS Norman had already pushed it open. Lydia took her hands off the keyboard. Daniel crouched down, trying to make himself less visible.

DS Norman's enormous boots crossed the floor and his fury filled the room. 'What do you think you're doing? I don't even know where to start with this! Tampering with evidence, accessing Mr Baynton's private social media accounts, compromising a police cordon –'

'What are *you* doing here?' I blurted out.

'We came to collect you boys, to get your statement. And it's a good job we found you when we did.'

'We?' I watched in horror as Dad and Mr Scouter loomed through the door.

Oh.

'Hello, Jonathan,' was all Dad said. What he meant was: 'Wait until I get YOU home.'

'I am deeply disappointed in you three.' Mr Scouter's face was a dark shade and he was breathing heavily through his bristling moustache. 'I thought I'd made it clear that the police were taking good care of the investigation? You obviously need *several* weeks of detention to drive that message home.'

I tried to feel pleased. The plan to get into deep, deep trouble was succeeding. I thought about summoning the baddest attitude I could, but Mr Scouter's rage kept me quiet.

'And who is this young lady?' DS Norman said.

'I'm Lydia,' she said, crossing her arms and staring him right back in the eye.

'Well, Lydia, can I suggest we give you a lift home? I'm going to have to speak to your parents.'

Lydia tried to charm her way out of it. 'Oh, that's

not necessary! I'm completely safe walking, and I swear, cross my heart and hope to die, that I will never look at someone else's Facebook account ever again . . .'

'I could take you to the police station to give you a formal warning, if you prefer? No? Good – now, what's your address?'

DS Norman was like a teacher but worse. Teachers can't chuck you in jail. I was so glad he didn't know we'd sneaked into Mr Baynton's house on Tuesday.

'I will see you off the premises,' Mr Scouter said, in a voice that promised us he wouldn't forget about the detentions. 'I'm so sorry, Detective Sergeant, to have let you down. I genuinely believed these boys to be suffering from stress. It appears they were more interested in playing detective.'

None of us looked at each other as we walked through the school and back to the car park in silence. Dad walked right beside me, oozing disapproval. I tried to be pleased about it. Daniel's feet dragged, but Lydia kept her arms crossed the whole way, keeping up the haughty attitude I knew (and was maybe starting, unwillingly, to admire).

'Well, DS Norman, I'm sure we will speak again. Please do feel free to give these children whatever official warnings they deserve …' Mr Scouter's voice trailed off as a very smart blue Mercedes swished into the car park.

Mrs Scouter popped her head out of the window as she drew the car to a halt beside us. 'What's all this?' she asked her husband. 'Don't tell me the police are making another arrest?'

I couldn't tell whether she was joking or not. I didn't find it very funny, anyway, nor did DS Norman.

'We've just discovered these three breaching a police cordon, madam, and I'm on my way to interview two of them about what they witnessed on Tuesday. If you will excuse us, we'd better be on our way.'

Mrs Scouter nodded. 'Of course, officer. Andrew, darling, I've brought back some of the VAT invoices. I don't suppose you've heard anything from the hospital about dear Millie?'

'Nothing. But I assume no news is good news.' Mr Scouter turned back towards the school as his wife manoeuvred her amazing car into the nearest parking space. I made a mental note to start paying attention in maths, if that was what an accountant drove.

We all crammed into the less impressive patrol car, Dad in the front with DS Norman and the three of us strapped tightly into the back. As he started the engine, we could hear the police radio, too faint to make out words but loud enough to remind us how official it all was.

I nudged Daniel. 'Why are you so quiet?' I whispered.

'Ghay'cha',' was all Daniel said. It sounded like it might be a Klingon swear word.[26]

'I'll drop you off first, Lydia, and then I can speak to you boys back at the station.' DS Norman signalled left. 'I've spoken to your mother on the phone, Daniel, and we've arranged that Mr Archer here will be your supervising adult for the purposes of the official statement.' DS Norman's face flashed across the rear-view mirror. 'Don't look so worried. She knows you're OK.'

Daniel tried to smile. It came out wrong.

Lydia was sunk into her seat, gazing out at the hedges and lamp posts flashing past the window.

26 It definitely is.

'You OK?' I muttered.

'No,' she replied, not even bothering to turn her head. 'Sucks to be me.'

I suppressed a twinge of guilt. The ideal outcome for me might actually turn out pretty bad for these two. But it wasn't all my fault. I hadn't made them break into the PE office, after all. Or hack into the computer.

We parked up outside the neat bungalow. A couple of neighbours' curtains moved – I bet they didn't get squad cars down Rounceval Street very often.

DS Norman pulled himself out of the driving seat and opened Lydia's door for her.

'You lot stay here. Won't be long.'

We watched as he rang the doorbell.

Lydia's gran opened the door and staggered backwards at the sight of her granddaughter in the company of a large grim-faced police officer. She beckoned them in quickly, looking left and right to check who was watching.

I winced. Poor Lydia.

'Who's the girl, then?' Dad asked, as Lydia's front door clicked shut.

'Lydia? None of your business.'

Dad took a sharp breath in. 'That attitude's not going to do you *any* favours.' I was lucky – at that moment his phone rang. He looked at the caller display. '*Humph*. I need to take this, it's work. Don't think for one second our conversation's over though, Jonathan.' He picked up the call and started to mutter about formaldehyde and casket linings.

Daniel continued to stare out of the window. I moved over to Lydia's empty seat.

Five minutes passed. I reckoned Lydia's gran would be hitting the roof. Lydia would be lucky to be allowed out of the house for school, let alone to continue investigating the case. It looked like Daniel and I were on our own again, but at least we had another lead now. Mr Muscle, aka Stan Waldron.

I tried to ignore the thrill I'd got out of our successes – finding the filing-cabinet keys in Mr Baynton's drawer, crossing off leads from our suspects list, breaking and entering the PE office, the feeling we were actually pulling off this investigation for real. But I had to remind myself *how guilty Lois Baynton looked*. After all, getting to the truth wasn't exactly the reason I was here.

I looked at the back of Dad's neck. He and Mum were definitely not going to be able to ignore this.

I had disappointed them plenty. I just hoped I'd done enough to get them to pull me out of Hanbridge High and take us all back to Grensham. And that I wasn't grounded for the next six million years – I needed a game of basketball with my mates, stat.

DS Norman came striding out of Lydia's house, rubbing the back of his neck, looking a bit flustered. The front door slammed behind him. As he got into the car, he glanced back at us.

'Right, that's one warning given. We'll go and get your statement recorded, and then I'll take you home, Daniel, and have a word with your mum, if she's up to it.'

They put us in a little interview room and brought Dad a cup of tea. We had to make do with tap water. There was one of those big two-way mirrors on the wall; I wondered if people were listening behind it, just like in *Brooklyn Nine-Nine*.

DS Norman interviewed Daniel and me together, with Dad sitting in as our Responsible Adult. We told DS Norman all the same stuff we'd told Mr Scouter the day before, plus the bit about finding the newspaper, and then about Stan Waldron's Facebook message to Mr Baynton. He listened carefully and wrote it all down.

'Well, that's clear enough. Now explain exactly *why* I found you looking at Mr Baynton's personal social media account?'

Dad refolded his arms and stared at me, in a *you're-grounded* sort of way.

I looked at Daniel. He was no use. His eyes had that kind of blank look you get when you've turned all the lights off and gone home early.

I didn't know what Lydia had told the police already.

The seconds ticked by.

I decided to fall back on that surly and uncooperative thing I'd been doing a lot since we moved to Hanbridge. 'Just being nosy. Wanted to know who might have killed him. We *were* the ones who found him, after all.' I shrugged, like I was bored of the conversation, and scratched at a blue mark on the table.

Dad took a loud breath in.

'This is a murder investigation, Jonathan,' DS Norman said. He put down his pen and leaned against the back of his chair, his dark brown eyes boring into mine. 'I would have thought you two, more than anyone, would understand how serious that is. Yes, you saw his body. I *suppose* I can understand that might have made you a bit curious, but it's up to the police, not a trio of school kids, to make sure the killer is brought to justice.'

I was desperate to know if they had anything on Stan Waldron before we'd told them about his message, and ask what they were doing about it if they did. But I didn't dare speak. DS Norman's eyes moved from my face to look at Daniel's thin white hands, clasped tightly together on the desk in front of him. I couldn't tell if Daniel was even listening.

'As your headteacher has already issued you with a reasonable punishment, i.e. detention, I am giving you an *in*formal warning to stay out of Mr Baynton's affairs. No hacking into computers, no poking around, no nothing. Let us do our job. A murder investigation is no place for juveniles. Your behaviour was totally unacceptable, and I won't overlook it a second time.'

Dad looked meaningfully at me. I knew I was going to hear a little more about my behaviour before the end of the day.

***

I was right.

He started as soon as we walked through the front

door. It was 8:30 and I hadn't had anything to eat since lunchtime. I was surprised I hadn't fainted from starvation already. Mum was upstairs singing Max to sleep, so at least I didn't get both of them at once.

'You and that boy – you stay out of police business – do you understand? This is not like you, Jonathan! What's going on? I can't believe DS Norman just walked in and caught you red-handed like that.'

'Yeah,' I said. 'Rookie mistake. He won't catch us again.' I was being funny, obviously, but Dad had never had much of a sense of humour.

'Don't you *dare* try anything like that again! If that Daniel – or the girl, Lorraine was it – are a bad influence, then I suggest you find someone else to hang around with.'

I was tempted to tell him that Jayden and Kinsey would do fine . . . but Dad didn't let me get a word in. 'This is a new start, Jonathan, and you need to make sure you don't end up regretting the choices you make.' And blah blah blah.

I admit I flinched a bit when some spittle actually flew out of Dad's mouth, but this kind of reaction was what I wanted.

I definitely didn't cry.

28

Friday 16 May, 7.45 a.m.

My house

I was just getting out of the shower next morning
when the doorbell rang.

'Jonathan,' Mum called, 'it's your friends. Here
before breakfast, very early, I think, for school.' Her
tone was highly disapproving.

Friends? My mind briefly flashed to Jay and
Kinsey, but obviously, nah. I'd tried both *Minecraft*
and the Discord chat last night to try and catch up
with them all, but I didn't seem to have access to
either of them any more. It gave me a really queasy
feeling when I thought about it.

'Just a minute!'

I threw my shirt and trousers on and thundered down the stairs.

'QUIETLY! You're like a parade of elephants. You should be on your best behaviour after yesterday's unacceptable activities,' she scolded as she walked back to the kitchen.

Why are adults so predictable?

Lydia certainly isn't. She and Daniel stood in the hall with a big black-and-white dog. He was dribbling on my school shoes, so I picked them up quick. Dad would go nuclear if they got chewed.

'Hi,' I said.

Daniel smiled mutely.

'Hi yourself.' Lydia sniffed. 'Gran let me out to walk Bingo before school. I'm not supposed to speak to either of you ever again. But I'm still, like, totally in. We've got new leads to follow up, so I think we'd better skive today.'

I reached out and shut the kitchen door. This was not a conversation Mum should hear. 'Skive? We could. Mr Scouter is on our case already, though, even if the police don't catch us again.'

'Give over! I'm in detention all the time. No one appreciates my natural genius round here. It's no big deal. And Daniel says no one at the station seemed interested in Stan Waldron. Or Ms Zheng, or Mrs Fustemann in hospital.'

'True,' I said, seriously tempted but holding back. In theory, even more detention was exactly what the doctor ordered – we might even get suspended. But as useful and interesting as the police station had been, I didn't completely fancy another visit.

'Jonathan – we're running out of time. Mum had a really bad night after that officer spoke to her yesterday,' Daniel said, with a grimace.

'What do you mean?' Lydia was right on it.

'Nothing – just, we should get on,' Daniel muttered.

I had a mental flashback to that yoga advert in Mr Baynton's hand. Daniel was so not going to cope when Lois Baynton turned out to be guilty.

'D'you think we should follow through on the Waldron clue, then?' Lydia turned from Daniel to me.

I did, although I was torn after Dad's earbashing. I hadn't slept too great. But Plan B was finally working. No doubt Mum and Dad had been talking all night about how much worse I was behaving since we left Grensham.

'Maybe . . . or maybe we should go to school and grill Ms Zheng again. Clearly she knows something we don't.' *And that way she might report us to Mr Scouter and give us more punishments.*

'Jonathan, this is a really important clue! We can't just ignore it. Stan Waldron threatened our murder victim!'

I sighed. 'OK. I guess we owe it to the cause of justice.' And the cause of me getting my life back. I mentally shook myself. I had to keep on making the riskiest choices.

'Well then, you'd better finish getting dressed so we can get going. They won't notice we're missing until registration, but the more time we can give ourselves the better.'

'What does the school do if you don't turn up?' Daniel had clearly never bunked off before. Bit like me.

'Someone in the office calls your dad or your gran or whoever. And then *they* come looking for you. We might be able to fake a call on the way to the High Street to put school off, but if they send Gran an acknowledgement text, we're stuffed. So let's go, go, go!'

I ran upstairs and finished adding socks, tie and a blazer to my outfit. My parents were going to be well unhappy when they got that phone call from school.

Which was *good*. Of course it was.

'See you tonight, Mum.' I squeezed past the others and stepped into the kitchen to grab a banana for breakfast.

'What's going on? You're not normally leaving until twenty past eight. I will not be pleased if more mischief is on the cards. No terrible catastrophes, please. Perhaps you should not be spending more time with these new companions today?' Mum would have started a proper interrogation, but for once, Max did something useful and spat porridge down his *Mumma's Best Boy* bib. It distracted Mum long enough for me to get out.

There was no time to lose, except that Lydia had to take that slobbery dog back. I ate my banana while Daniel and I skulked behind a hedge at the end of Rounceval Street. I could have done with a piece of toast too.

'So, about Gavin,' Daniel said.

'Ooh, yes? Did you speak to your mum?' I said, mouth full.

'Yeah. She was pretty upset, unsurprisingly, when I came home in a squad car. Thinks the police are going to call in social services to check up on her parenting. I can't let this go on much longer,

Jonathan, she'll get herself into a terrible state. But there was something. Apparently, she'd heard from another of Lois's friends about Gavin.'

'Amazing.' Daniel's mum had guts, that was for sure. 'What did she say?'

'It's a dead end. Gavin's been in Yorkshire working as a kitchen fitter. Hasn't been back to Bristol for a couple of months.'

'Damn. Did you find out what the fight was about between him and Mr B?'

'Money, Mum reckoned. Lending and borrowing, but she wasn't sure of the details.'

That was disappointing, but not surprising. Another name to scrub off the list.

'Mum had a message from Lois's solicitor yesterday too. Apparently, the case for the defence is not looking very promising. They haven't got CCTV footage from the school – someone turned the cameras off just after six p.m., *after* Lois spoke to Mrs Fustemann. And a couple of clients from Lois's yoga class have testified that she's extremely physically strong . . .'

I didn't know what to say. She wasn't sounding very innocent. Not that Daniel wanted to hear it.

'Any progress on the stuff we found in the filing

cabinet?' I asked. I'd let my mind dwell on the notebook a number of times; it was a fascinating puzzle for which I didn't have all the pieces. 'Do you think it could be smuggling? Like, dates and amounts of dodgy products, beer or cigarettes or something?'

Daniel shook his head. 'I'm not sure that adds up. Cos there are fractions, aren't there – one sixth of something and three eighths . . . no idea what those might refer to, but they can't be beer. Maybe the book's got something to do with Stan Waldron, though.'

Lydia rounded the corner, dog-free, and Daniel set off at a fast walk, his trousers riding up to expose his Mr Spock socks.

'I looked up Cash4Cheques last night,' he said. 'The shop's open eight till eight on a weekday. Don't know if Mr Waldron'll be there himself, though.'

'Sweet.'

I looked over my shoulder a few times as we headed towards the High Street, half expecting to see DS Norman's angry face, or Lydia's gran creeping up on us wagging a painted fingernail. Unfortunately, that meant I was looking the wrong way when Tyler Jenkins came scuffing down his front drive and stopped in the middle of the pavement.

'L-look who it is,' he sneered. 'The ginger ninja, new boy and the dweeb. What are you l-lot up to?'

Lydia put away the phone she'd got out, no doubt to call the school. She looked Tyler straight in the eye. 'Popping to the shops before school. Which slime pit did you crawl out of?'

'Now, n-now. Not my fault you're the saddos round here, no need to t-take it out on me. You've m-managed that all by yourselves, with your w-weird n-nerdy obsessions.'

Daniel looked kind of stricken, like he wanted to curl up under a hedge. Lydia opened her mouth to slash and burn Tyler back, but he hadn't quite finished.

'You ought to give yourselves a n-name, now you're hanging out together. What about The Geek Squad? Or, how'sabout, Hanbridge D-dorks and Losers Club.' Tyler nearly fell over, he was so amused by himself.

I suddenly found I'd had enough.

'I'd rather be a dork or a loser than a spineless *scumbag*,' I said.

I walked on quickly, hoping the others were right behind me. And that Tyler wasn't.

'We're a TEAM, not a club,' I heard Daniel mutter. I tried not to smile.

'You're going to l-live to regret that, mind,' I heard Tyler call, but he didn't chase us or throw any rocks.

I had a queasy feeling he might like his revenge served cold.

'OK,' said Lydia, and changed the subject, like Tyler didn't deserve any further attention. 'What did DS Norman say to your mum last night?' she asked Daniel. 'Gran didn't let him say much to her. She took one look at him and ripped into me. Apparently I'm just like my mother.'

Daniel looked puzzled. 'Because – you're a fan of water sports?'

Lydia screwed up her eyes in confusion. 'Water sports? What on earth . . . Ah! Surfing. Yes. No, not like that. Like, being badly behaved.'

'Oh. Well, DS Norman just warned Mum to keep an eye on me. But she's not a big fan of authority figures . . .' Daniel stopped. His cheeks flushed.

Lydia raised an eyebrow. 'Don't worry, I'm not going to ask.'

We passed the vet and the hardware store.

Cash4Cheques was over the road, between a kebab shop and the Redfern Bakery.

'Who's going to do the talking?' I asked. I won't lie, I was jumpy. This Stan bloke had looked like a wall of muscle.

'I'll talk,' Lydia volunteered immediately, to no one's surprise.

Lydia led the way, pushing the door, which beeped loudly. Cash4Cheques was a weird kind of shop; just an empty space, with a glass hatch on one wall next to a scratched-up door – labelled, very clearly, PRIVATE.

It was dusty and smelled of sweaty gym socks. A bored-looking woman sat behind the glass, chewing gum and reading the new *Gazette*. She looked up as we nudged each other nearer the hatch.

'What d'you lot want?'

'We're looking for Mr Waldron,' Lydia said in her best good-girl voice.

'Over-eighteens only.' The woman tried to out-stare Lydia.

Lydia was way ready for that.

'We don't want to speak to him about cash. And I don't even own a cheque book. We would like to speak to him about a . . . personal matter.'

The woman raised an eyebrow. But she pulled a phone out of her fleece pocket and dialled a number.

'Stan? It's Polly. You got visitors downstairs.' She chuckled. 'No, nothing to worry about. Just some kids; prob'ly want a donation to the Brownies or something.' She grinned nastily at Lydia.

The woman put the phone down on the counter. 'You can go on up.' She pointed towards the PRIVATE sign on the door to the right.

'Thank you very much,' Lydia said.

The door squealed horribly as she pushed it open. We looked up at the narrow splintery staircase towering ahead. It did not look inviting.

'I'll go first,' Lydia said, after a few awkward seconds.

Daniel nodded gratefully and I patted Lydia on the shoulder. 'Nice one.'

It was quiet, apart from the creaking steps as we climbed. None of us spoke.

We were just reaching the top when an arm shot out from the left and stopped Lydia in her tracks.

Daniel screamed.

I didn't, mainly because I was trying to stop myself from falling back down.

The arm was followed by a huge mountain of man. Stan Waldron was every bit as muscly as he looked on Facebook, even in stripy pyjamas and a fluffy dressing gown.

'Who are you, then?' His voice was deep and gravelly.

He scratched at his stubbly jaw and looked from Daniel to Lydia and on to me. I was *completely* chill, obviously.

Lydia recovered the quickest. 'Good morning, Mr Waldron. We apologize for our early call, but we had a question or two that you might be able to help us with.'

'About what?' Mr Waldron looked puzzled.

'Well . . .' Lydia's voice petered out. My turn.

'Mr Baynton,' I said, louder than I meant to.

'You what?' Stan Waldron glowered. 'That blimmin' nit? He's gone and got himself killed, and I'm out of pocket. So unless you've come to pay his debts, I ain't got nothing to say.'

'We found his body, Mr Waldron. We're trying to find out . . . who might have had a motive . . . or . . .' Daniel's voice trailed off.

Stan Waldron loomed, horribly, as he realized what Daniel had said. I took a step down.

'I hope very much you are not accusin' me of anything, sunshine . . .' His enormous fist was clenched and he lifted it slightly until it was level with Daniel's nose.

'No, no, nothing like that!'

Lydia and I both started explaining at the same time.

'We are talking to all local business people who might have had dealings with him . . .'

'Your name just came up and we wondered if you could tell us . . .'

I could feel my blazer getting tighter and my armpits starting to prickle.

Stan Waldron made a *zip* noise and pulled his fingers across his lips. 'I need coffee before I'm goin' to understand what you lot are on about.' He lifted his shoulders up into a muscle-bound shrug. 'Why don't you follow me. I'll be in a better mood once I'm caffeinated.'

We all gave each other a look. I could tell Daniel was having many thoughts, but I knew he wouldn't turn tail. Not with the threat of social services breathing down his mum's neck.

I would have been OK to tiptoe back down the stairs and get the hell out of it. But . . .

'Come on,' Lydia said.

So on we went.

Friday 16 May, 8.30 a.m.

Stan Waldron's flat

Stan was standing in his small yellow kitchen, pouring muesli into a huge bowl. He poured half a pint of milk on top and stabbed his spoon at us.

'You, girl. Sit over there and tell me what's going on.'

Lydia sat down obediently on the far side of the table. Daniel leaned against the fridge, and I squeezed into a small space beside the door.

The kettle behind Stan was coming to the boil, so Lydia waited until he'd filled his World's Best Dad mug and sat himself down.

'I apologize if we've caused any offence,' Lydia began. 'But we are looking into Mr Baynton's death, because the police have decided not to bother.'

'I thought they arrested his wife?'

Lydia shot Daniel a dirty look. 'Well, we are pretty certain she's not guilty.'

'So? What's that got to do with me?' Stan mumbled through a mouthful of muesli.

'It's –' Daniel butted in, but Stan looked up quickly and shook his head.

'She's talking,' he said, pointing his spoon at Lydia.

Daniel went a bit paler, if that was possible, and shut his mouth.

Lydia smiled smoothly. 'To be honest, we were a bit ... naughty, and had a quick look at Mr Baynton's computer. There were some messages from you – you seemed to know him ...'

I admired Lydia's diplomatic language.

'Yeah, I knew the nasty little toerag. I could tell you a few things about Ollie Baynton that'd make your hair curl.' Stan took a swig of his coffee, eyes fixed on Daniel. 'I've got no reason to go around telling my business to a bunch of nosy kids. But *you* look like you got good reasons to be here, boy. So *you* tell me what they are, then I'll decide what I feel like saying.'

I could see the hairs on Daniel's arm standing up.

'I don't . . . What do you mean?' Daniel said.

Stan Waldron's spoon flashed in the air again. 'The lass is doing this for kicks, that's blimmin' obvious, and the quiet lad by the door isn't even sure why he's here at all, but *you* . . .' He dropped the spoon into his bowl with a wet clink. 'You've got something to lose. Tell me about it.'

I wondered whether being the 'quiet lad' was a good thing or not. And I was pretty sure I did know why I was there, actually. Daniel's desperation must have been sending out confusing vibes.

Daniel glanced at Lydia. She folded her arms.

'Looks like it's time to spill the beans, Daniel,' she said.

'But . . . it's private.'

Lydia shrugged. 'You've got two choices: tell Mr Waldron here what's going on, or we go back to school and let the police deal with this their way. Up to you.'

Daniel looked at me with big, worried eyes, trying to transmit an SOS by telepathy. I hated it when he did that. Why couldn't Daniel ever think up his own flaming lie?

'You should tell them about how your mum's a bit unwell just now, and the police have arrested her best friend, and how upset she is about Lois.' I raised my eyebrows, and Daniel's scrunched-up face relaxed very slightly.

'OK. So, Lois – Mrs Baynton – she's been my mum's best friend for years and years. And the police have gone and arrested her –'

'On purely circumstantial evidence,' I dropped in.

'Yeah, she wouldn't hurt a fly! She's a lovely person and she totally doesn't deserve to go to jail.'

Stan Waldron's large face turned on his thick neck to take us both in. 'I'd stake a few quid that's not the whole story. But I reckon you're telling the truth as far as it goes. So I'll tell you this.' He got up and put his bowl in the sink. The muscles in his arms flexed and lengthened as he turned the hot tap on. Above the sound of the sink filling with water Stan said, 'Ollie Baynton. Not my favourite customer. He was a regular down at my mate Craig's betting shop on the corner. Not just football and horses, either – he'd take a punt on anything.'

'How do you mean?' Daniel asked.

I flinched as Stan Waldron plonked his clean bowl heavily on the draining rack.

'What I mean is, he'd put money on which duck would eat the bread first. Literally anything. Thing is, PE teachers don't earn enough for him to lose as often as he did. He was a rubbish gambler.'

'So . . . he borrowed money from you?' Lydia's whipcrack brain jumped to the right conclusion immediately.

Stan Waldron nodded. 'That he did. He owed me over seven grand.'

Seven thousand pounds? That's not pocket money. You can buy a small car for that.

'And he was late paying me back. So . . . I took matters into my own hands. The police have already been round and asked me about it. And I'm afraid I might have put ideas into his wife's head . . .' Stan sighed.

'Lois?' Daniel was right on it. 'What did you say?'

Stan Waldron went slightly pink. 'I'd had enough. Ollie was ignoring calls and texts. So I went round his house a few nights ago. Turned out he was down the hockey club, reffing a match. But she was in.'

'What happened?' I felt like it was my turn to ask a question.

'I asked when I was going to get my cash. She didn't know anything about it. So I ended up telling her about his gambling. She was mad as hell, especially when I said how much he owed me. I expect that's why she killed him, probably.'

'She didn't! She never would!' Daniel was actually shouting at the beefiest man in the world.

I tried to hide behind the kitchen door. Everything Stan was saying was reinforcing my private suspicions about Lois's guilt.

'I've known her all my life, she's kind and caring!' Daniel ranted on.

Stan put his huge palms face down on the table and leaned into them. 'Yeah, she looked like a nice girl to me. But when it comes to love and money . . .' He sucked his teeth. 'People can get really, really crazy. Do stuff that's completely out of character. You might have to get used to that fact.'

Stan Waldron made a good point, I thought.

Lydia frowned. 'Can you tell us anything else that might help?'

'Well –' Stan scratched his head – 'he was pushy. Wanted to be the bigshot, ideally at Bristol Rovers. And he reckoned refereeing was going to get him there. He'd done a few games down at the netball club, and more for the Bristol hockey team. I think he was trying to, whatsit-called, *network*, get to know anyone locally who could recommend him for bigger and better things.'

I looked quickly at Lydia and Daniel. *Was that a new lead?*

'Well, that is certainly something for us to think about, isn't it, boys? We are very grateful for your time, Mr Waldron. We'd better leave you to your day,' Lydia said politely. Her gaze met mine and she nodded towards the door.

Guess that's a lead, then.

She got up from the table. 'Come on, Daniel, Jonathan.'

Stan Waldron was taken aback. 'That's enough, is it? You don't want to interrogate me about my latest tax return or anything? Oh, well. Bye then, kids. It's been . . . interesting.'

I followed Daniel and Lydia carefully down the narrow stairs and through the door to the shop. There was a queue of miserable-looking people waiting to speak to the woman behind the glass.

I wouldn't be going back there in a hurry.

30

Friday 16 May, 9.15 a.m.

The Nook Cafe

Lydia looked at her watch. 'Right. It's nine fifteen. We better get out of sight in case school's rung the olds already.'

Daniel pointed across the road to the coffee shop. 'We could sit in there for a bit. Does anyone have any money?'

Lydia nodded. 'I've got enough for a cup.'

She pushed open the door to the Nook Cafe. It was identical to all the coffee shops I've ever sat in. Dreary magazines in one corner, toddlers wailing at their parents in boredom, lists of weird and expensive hot drinks.

Lydia went to the counter to order a milky mocha, while Daniel and I found a leather sofa to sit on. The stained cushion under my elbow said HOME IS WHERE THE HEART IS in pastel pinks. The floor was slightly sticky.

Lydia sat down, and we waited in awkward silence as she sipped her hot, sweet drink.

'So. Was that any use to us?' Lydia was finally ready to chair the meeting.

'I suppose Mr Baynton's gambling was news,' Daniel said, leaning on one elbow and gazing at the salt cellar on the table in front of us.

'And we didn't know about Lois finding out he was in massive debt.' I thought I ought to mention it. It was looking even more obvious that Daniel's lovely Lois was not innocent.

'It *wasn't* Lois. It must have been someone else. Maybe he owed money to more than one person?' Daniel said. 'Gavin – he was on our list, remember – he'd argued with Mr Baynton about money, though that lead's fallen through too. Maybe he borrowed money from another teacher?'

'We can't really rule Mr Waldron out yet,' Lydia pointed out. 'He didn't give us an alibi or anything. Just took it for granted that we believed his story about talking to Mrs Baynton and left it at that. He's definitely strong enough to kill Mr B with his bare hands.'

Daniel sat up. 'That's true,' he said.

'Hold on, hold on. He wouldn't have told us *anything* if he's at all guilty,' I said. 'He didn't need to tell us about Mr Baynton owing him money, or that he'd been round to his house looking for him. And he said he'd talked to the police already about that.'

'Hmm. And he wouldn't have been with Mrs Fustemann when she got pushed down the stairs, either,' Lydia said. As if we'd decided that was definitely not an accident.

'Who else is still unaccounted for? Ms Zheng is unlikely cos of the timings of her tweets, but she had something on him she was threatening him with. There *must* be a link between this reffing stuff he was doing and the message she sent him,' Daniel said.

That same itch in my brain came back. There was something about those initials Ms Zheng had mentioned, BTHC, and the information Stan had given us, that made me think about the notebook we'd found in Mr Baynton's filing cabinet. What was the link? I thought about each column I'd seen, the dates and all those figures. Could they relate to sums of money? I racked my brains . . . and it finally dawned on me. I'd seen lists of initials followed by numbers like that in the boring financial Sunday papers Mum reads – she said they were company share prices. Was it possible to buy bits of shares, *fractions* of them maybe, instead of whole ones? Having seen the contents of his designer wardrobe, it sounded like something Mr Baynton would do, to try and be like one of those flash money traders on Wall Street. Maybe *that* was what his notebook was referring to?

I contemplated suggesting we go to Daniel's house to take another look at it, but there really didn't seem to be much point. Even if it had something to do with Mr Baynton's refereeing jobs, Lois was still the only viable suspect at the end of the day. We were just going through the motions.

'. . . I just don't think Ms Zheng's got it in her to commit murder. She's too law-abiding,' Lydia was saying.

Daniel slumped further into the sofa, sliding down until his knees were higher than his chin. 'So, back to the drawing board, then. We don't know anyone else who might have had a motive! Unless Mr Packington or Mr Chayning is guilty? They've not come up since that staff meeting, anyway.'

'Why don't we update the list?' I decided, pulling it out of my coat pocket.

Suspects	Timeline	Evidence
~~1. MRS FUSTEMANN: ROW~~ • Second victim?? • No contact via Facebook ~~2. MS ZHENG: FEUD~~ • Alibi – Social media? • Cagey about time of crime • Was investigating refereeing . . . 3. MR PACKINGTON: BULLYING ETC • Too lazy to bother? 4. MR CHAYNING: IPADS(!) • Unlikely!	• Stan tells Lois about gambling debt • Mr Baynton and Lois argue 5.30 pm • Mr Baynton back at school/other teachers leave by 6.00 pm • CCTV off at 6.00 pm • Ms Zheng tweeting at 6.17–6.25 pm • Governors' meeting 7.00–8.30 pm • School locked by 9.00 pm • 9.00 pm + Mrs F at cinema with sister?	• Shed open • Strangled by hand • Photo of Mrs Fustemann in local paper • Second murder attempt on Mrs F? • Notebook • Money issues – Mr Baynton had gambling debt and was borrowing from friends/Stan • Refereeing – does that mean something?

5. ~~MR FRANTOCK/~~ ~~MISS BLACK-~~ ~~DUDLEY: MYSTERY~~ ~~RE. ALIBIS~~ • In secret relationship 6. ~~MRS SUDELY:~~ ~~DODGY CONVO~~ ~~WITH MR SINCLAIR~~ • Alibi for Mrs F's accident/D o E cover-up • Lydia has explanation for their conversation 7. ~~GAVIN: FIGHT~~ 8. ~~STAN WALDRON:~~ ~~FB MESSAGE~~ • Told a good story – didn't have to explain • Mentioned refereeing		

We studied the remaining names.

'Well, what about this refereeing?' I asked. 'If Ms Zheng was interested in it too, it must be significant?'

'Bristol hockey team's pitch is just down the road – we used to practise there for league games sometimes, back in primary. I guess we could go and ask around, see if we can turn up any new info? It's that or go back to school.' Daniel gave a shrug.

'Right, then! Let's go,' Lydia said. She slugged the last of her coffee and swung open the cafe door only to slam it shut a split second later.

'Gran!' Lydia stood with her back to the door.

'What? Where?' Daniel said.

'In the car, sweeping the streets for me. I don't think she saw me, though.'

Damn. We'd forgotten to call the school.

'If we go now, she'll be at the end of this road or on to the next one. If we wait, she might circle back,' Daniel said, being cool and logical for once. Maybe the Spock socks were having a magical effect on his brain.

Me? I was sweating.

Lydia cracked open the door. Then she shoved me up to the gap. 'Can you see her?' she whispered. 'She'll be in the worst mood. I'll be grounded for months.'

The door frame dug into my cheek. 'Blue Honda?'

'No. She has a silver Renault. Small-ish.'

'Can't see it,' I said.

'OK . . . go.'

We jogged along the High Street, heads down, Lydia not daring to look around. I didn't have a clue where the hockey club was so I had to lag behind the other two. Which was good, in a way, because I was the one who heard the squeaky brakes of a silver Renault Clio pausing at the end of the side street, right behind me.

The other two didn't spot it, hurrying along past the newsagent's, but I knew Lydia's hair would be a dead giveaway. So I did something instinctive. I took a step backwards, so I was in front of the passenger-door window, blocking the driver's view down the street.

Yes, with my bum.

Clearly, my booty did not ring any bells with Lydia's gran. She turned right instead of left and I breathed out painfully.

Then I ran to catch up.

31

Friday 16 May, 9.40 a.m.

Hanbridge High Street

Lydia and Daniel turned down a side road signposted LOCAL AUTHORITY ALLOTMENTS – NO THROUGH ROAD. Ahead were a bunch of marked-out pitches behind a long, low building. BRISTOL TOWN HOCKEY CLUB was painted in high purple letters along the side.

Immediately I felt like an idiot. 'BTHC, guys – from Ms Zheng's email? It's right there in front of us. Bristol Town Hockey Club!'

'Oh yes!' Lydia said. 'So this has GOT to mean something. How are we going to find out what?'

Floodlights dotted the pitch corners, and a solitary Range Rover was parked outside.

'If there's someone here, we can ask,' Daniel said. 'We'll need a cover story. I could be a fan trying to get some autographs, maybe?'

I snorted. 'Like people want autographs from regional hockey teams.'

We stepped into the small car park. At one end there was a large board screwed to the wall, under the giant purple letters.

'What does it say on that noticeboard?' I said.

'Lost cat. That's no help.' Daniel pointed to a badly photocopied picture of a grey tabby.

Lydia stretched out and touched the poster below it. 'Junior members try-outs. Ms Zheng mentioned something about that last week, in PE.'

I carried on reading the small print aloud.

'*BTHC seeks new players to join their squad. Boys and girls aged eleven to sixteen with an interest in teamwork and competitive play should attend our open try-outs on Saturday, 25 May. For more information speak to our junior squad coach, Dorothy L. Merchant.*'

'Perfect!' Lydia said. 'I'll pop in and enquire.'

'Why you?' I lifted an eyebrow. 'It did say boys *or* girls. We could all be interested, couldn't we?'

Lydia clapped me firmly between the shoulder blades. Ouch. 'Good point, Jonathan! Did you play hockey in your old school?'

'Yeah. I was OK – mainly goalkeeping.' I didn't say how boring I thought hockey was.

'Dammit. Hanbridge needs a decent keeper but it's a girls' league.'

'I don't think I've ever played hockey.' Daniel blinked. He wasn't going to be very convincing.

'Let me and Lydia do the talking,' I suggested as I pulled open the uPVC door at the back of the building.

A bell tinkled in a room nearby. We stood awkwardly together in a wide corridor alongside framed photographs of past captains dressed in team kit – variations on green, white and purple.

'Comin'!' came a female voice from the room. A cheerful older woman popped her head out of the doorway to our left. 'You lookin' fur me, loves?' she said. She had brown curly hair and dark brown skin, and she was non-ironically wearing an 80s-style tracksuit, as if she'd just finished a Jazzercise session. Her accent was the broadest Bristolian.

'Hi,' Lydia said in her best manner. 'We were just wondering about the junior try-outs . . .'

'Shouldn't you be up at the 'igh school?' the lady asked, looking us up and down curiously. ''Ere, there's no INSET today, is it?'

'No, not an INSET. There was – a leak. In the science labs. So we got a free period.' Daniel's improvisation impressed me. I nodded firmly and Lydia picked up the thread, nice and smooth.

'Yes, we thought we'd do something useful with the time instead of hanging out by the shops. Our friend here – Jon . . . ny, he's just moved to the area, and he's looking for somewhere to play. He's a great goalie. And I fancied a go at getting on the team too. I play for the school.'

The lady smiled. 'Well, that's mighty good news! I'm Miz Valda Campbell. I be the club administra'er.' She beckoned to us and we followed her into the admin office.

'Dorothy's not 'ere at the moment, but I can tell you a bit 'bout the team, an' costs an' that.' She was rummaging through piles of paper on her cramped desk. 'I'm sure I got some of th'information forms 'ere somewhere – you can take 'em now an' fill 'em in before try-outs on Sa'urday, if you like.'

She dumped a pile of booklets on the floor and then kicked them over as she opened drawer after drawer.

'Oh, don't worry about forms! Could you just tell us a bit about the club?' Lydia said.

'Well, what it is, yeah, the form tells you about the fees – we try not to make it too expensive, but it does cost a mean lot runnin' this place.' Valda Campbell sat down in her chair and looked at us. 'Trainin' is Fursday evenin' from six to eight and Sa'urday mornin' nine up until twelve. We're a serious club, mind – our seniors are top o' the league, and we got sev'ral players called up fur England next month. Iss pretty compet'tive,' she continued, looking at Daniel as he squeezed his bony hands together.

'Oh, Daniel's just come for the walk, haven't you?' Lydia breezed us out of trouble again.

'Could you give us a tour?' I said. I didn't have any good ideas about what to ask but I figured I'd have to bring Mr Baynton up at some point. It felt uncomfortable doing it in that little office.

Valda Campbell blinked. 'Yeah, I s'pose – yeah, I'll show you arr facili'ies, the changin' rooms an' the pitches an' that. Mind you – I don't s'pose you got long, 'ave you? If you've only got one free period?'

'No worries,' I said, before Daniel could speak. 'It was double science, so we've got a bit of time.'

She led us down a shiny corridor to two very uninteresting changing rooms. I rattled my brain trying to shake free something to ask.

Lydia was clearly doing the same. 'So when are the matches? Sundays?' she asked.

'Well, depends if iss a league game or a friendly . . .'

Miss Valda Campbell explained in detail. I felt Daniel turn and look at me. Why he couldn't ask something himself, I don't know.

Miss Campbell pushed open a door and we went outside.

'Err – did you know Mr Baynton, our PE teacher who – used to referee here sometimes?' I blurted the words out, feeling Daniel's gaze still on me. It instantly felt like a bad idea.

Miss Campbell turned round. Her face was less kind. ''E's barely cold, young man, I 'ope yer not 'ere lookin' for gossip . . . We 'ad someone else 'ere a couple days back, askin' about 'im. Short woman, askin' all sorts, she was, what dates he'd been reffin' and oo was 'is manager. T'wasn't seemly, not at all.'

We three shared a glance. *Ms Zheng*.

'Erm, so, did you tell her?' I asked.

'No, I did not!' said Miss Campbell. 'That there's none of anyone's business 'cept the club's.'

'No, of course not. We, we just ... wanted to express our condolences. We heard he was a really good referee.' Lydia tried to patch it up.

'I like your floodlights,' Daniel said in a small voice.

'Yes, they'm really useful in the winter.' Miss Campbell seemed to have lost interest in showing us the hockey pitches. 'Now.' She looked at her watch. 'D'you want me t'ave another go at findin' them forms ...?'

'Ummm, yes, please. Thank you,' Lydia said.

'Awright, then, wait 'ere and I'll bring 'em out in a minute.'

'Thank you!' we all chorused, like the harmless young boys and girl we were pretending to be.

As soon as she was out of sight, Lydia grabbed us both. 'Look,' she said and pointed towards a large display board on the rear side of the building. She dragged us towards it by our elbows. 'I recognize that face, don't you?'

The board showed photos of all the club VIPs. Both junior and senior captains were there, Miss Campbell, obviously, some bloke with a moustache the shape of a toothbrush . . .

And Mrs Fustemann.

Above her head was a big white label saying Club Treasurer.

'Well. There she is again,' I said.

We crowded round the board. Under the photo there was a phone number and some office hours listed for Saturday mornings.

'What do you think it means?' Daniel asked, glancing from me to Lydia.

'Mrs Fustemann is involved here, and so was Mr Baynton. That's got to be what they were arguing about – something to do with the club.' Lydia's voice rose.

'Who's arguin' 'bout wot?' Miss Campbell said sharply from the doorway behind us.

'Are those the forms? Thank you, Miss Campbell . . .' Lydia tried to snap back into super-nice mode. 'We'll take these back to school and get on with filling them out.'

'Wot you lookin' at? Oh, course, you'll know Millie Fustemann. We've got quite a number o' c'nections to 'anbridge 'igh.' She looked at Daniel. 'I don't s'pose you've 'eard any news this mornin'? 'Bout how she's doin', after 'er fall? We'd be lost without 'er 'ere.'

I thought I'd do some asking myself. 'So, Mrs Fustemann's your treasurer. Has she been involved with the club long?'

'Oh, the Collinses 'ave bin members of this club for years. In fact, they take it in turns to serve on the commi'ee. They're amazin', they are – put so much time an' effort into keeping us lot goin'.'

'Wait, who are the Collinses?' Lydia read my mind.

'The sisters – Millie, an' dear Felicity. They're not called Collins any more, o' course – they ain't been those names for twenty years o' more! Now, Felicity, she's married to –'

'Lydia Strong!' A loud and irritated voice came from behind the high back gate, just over to our left.

'Oo's that?' Miss Campbell pricked her ears.

Could we never catch a break? Lydia's gran was on our tail *again*.

'I heard your voice, young lady! Where are you?' Gran wasn't giving up easily.

Lydia rose up on tiptoes, whipping her head towards the sound. 'She's *just* there.'

We heard Gran's angry sniff right outside the gate. Bingo began barking with joy.

Lydia turned to me and Daniel and shoved us behind the building. 'Stay here. I'll deal with this.' She slipped through the gate and we heard her a second later.

'Gran! There you are!'

'What do you mean, there *I* am? Where do you think *you've* been, young lady? You are supposed to be at school, not hanging around Hanbridge like a waif or stray! I thought you were going to school early to revise for a test, and next thing I know you're missing!'

'Well, there was a problem with – with school. Tyler Jenkins was waiting outside the gates, and I thought he was going to beat me up for being a maths swot, so . . .'

I unfroze enough to look up, and saw Miss Valda Campbell listening, open-mouthed, to Lydia's lies.

32

Friday 16 May, 10.05 a.m.

Bristol Town Hockey Club

I went with my gut instinct.

I ran.

Miss Campbell might have hesitated for a moment, but like any adult faced with a kid running away she made a quick judgement – they must be up to mischief.

She chased me over the first pitch, leaping over the fence with surprising agility for a person of her age. I looked back quickly and saw Daniel standing like a statue by the wall, all confused and wide-eyed. Miss Campbell was gaining on me. I really wished I'd had that toast this morning.

I put on an extra spurt of speed. I'm quicker than any middle-aged adult, no matter how many retro workouts they'd done. I coasted past the floodlights at the rear of the clubhouse and doubled back round towards the front of the building. I was hoping Daniel would have the sense to walk towards the front entrance.

I rounded the corner of the clubhouse, knees pumping, as I tried to keep my lead.

Thank God, Daniel was just emerging. I grabbed his hand and pulled him out of the car park and on to the road. Left, back to the High Street or right, towards the allotments?

I figured there was more cover down in shed city. I could hear Miss Campbell's gasping breath and heavy feet just behind us.

'Come on, Daniel!' I kept hold of his sweaty hand and we sprinted. Appalled residents peeked through their windows as we hammered down past a rank of old stone cottages to the allotment gate. It was locked.

That didn't slow me down very much. I grabbed the rusty metal and hurdled it.

'Come on, Daniel!' It was turning into my catchphrase.

His thin face was screwed up with panic as it swivelled from me to Miss Campbell, making good progress along past the cottages. In our wake, dogs were barking, front doors were opening up and we were the centre of all that attention.

'Get yourself over here, now!' I was panicking too. I didn't want him blabbing if Miss Campbell got hold of him. That would be the end of our investigation – Lydia locked down by her gran, Daniel interrogated by Valda, and me? I didn't much fancy another shouting match with Dad right now, and I wasn't getting any better at sassing the teachers. I guess I'd end up skulking back to school and pretending I'd been trapped in a cupboard. I knew a good one, after all.

No way. Not yet.

I leaned over the fence and grabbed Daniel again, this time round the waist. With strength I probably got from pure fear I heaved him over the gate and on to my shoulder.

We sprawled on to the muddy ground as his weight overbalanced me.

'Down here!' I panted, sweating with effort. I'd been running hard – give me a break.

We scrambled into a ditch behind a pile of rotting

compost and lay down, accidentally picking a particularly brambly bit near the hedge as our hiding place. Daniel squealed as his head went right into a clump of nettles. I put my hand over his mouth to shut him up.

Not a second too soon: Miss Campbell reached the gate while Daniel's left foot was still out in the open.

We were *so* lucky. She was out of breath and fed up. She looked around for twenty seconds, max, holding on to her side like she had a stitch. Then she turned round and walked slowly back to the hockey club. Gossipy neighbours stopped her to ask for all the details.

I crossed my fingers that Lydia and her gran had already left.

I kept down for a minute, in case it was a trap. Daniel had gone kind of limp but I didn't dare take my hand off his face.

Until I got worried. Didn't fancy another murder scene. I released him and crawled back upright, trying not to breathe in the smell of mouldy vegetables from the compost heap.

His lily-white face stared up at me.

'Are we safe?' he whispered.

'Yeah. She's given up.'

I put out a hand and helped Daniel out of the ditch. He was shaking.

'You pushed me into a nettle,' he complained, lifting a dirty hand to rub at his pink ear.

'If I hadn't, Miss Campbell'd be marching you up the road, demanding you explain all our business.' I didn't have any sympathy to spare. Worries were crawling around my head like a nest of caterpillars.

'Let's find somewhere to sit down and have a think,' I said. 'I'd suggest one of those benches over there, but we probably shouldn't stay here for long in case Miss Campbell's called the cops on us, or someone in the cottages comes poking around to make sure we're not damaging their leeks.'

I closed my eyes, imagining for a couple of seconds how furious DS Norman might look if he turned up to find us knee deep in his case again. I kept struggling with mixed feelings about getting into bad trouble, now I knew how it actually felt.

'Let's go down by the river instead.' Daniel looked keen to leave the allotments too. 'There's a patch of trees just up the road where we can hide out.'

'OK.' I popped my head above the gate, to check if there were still witnesses hanging around. All was clear, so I helped Daniel climb back over, slightly more gently this time. I was feeling a bit puffed out. So far this morning we'd interrupted a giant's breakfast, sneaked into a hockey club under false pretences, dodged Lydia's gran, and been chased into a ditch. And it was only 10:15 a.m.

We walked away fast. Daniel led me through a gap in some brambles and more massive nettles at the side of the road. The trees were huge, leaning over my head and sprouting bright young leaves. It was cold and quiet, despite cars passing only a few metres away. I could hear the river, flowing fast, just as loud from the other direction.

Daniel pointed to a little hummock of grass between a group of what were probably oaks. The ground was littered with last autumn's leaves. We both sat down with a groan.

'So. Here we are,' I said, rubbing the sweat from my upper lip and wafting up my shirt to unstick it from my back.

'Do you think Lydia is OK?' Daniel had his eyes closed and he was leaning forward against his bent knees.

'Lydia can talk her way out of anything. Don't worry about her. We've got to think about us.' I broke off a bit of twig and scratched my shoe with it.

Daniel did this big sigh, like the end of the world was coming, then snapped his eyes open, pulling himself together a bit. 'I suppose we should recap. Mrs Fustemann came up again. She's got to be in it up to her neck.'

'We know Mr B was in debt. And Mrs Fustemann and her sister Felicity, whoever she is, the former Collins sisters, looked after the club's money, didn't they? Maybe there's something in that . . .'

'Yes.' Daniel's eyes opened wider as he stared up at me. 'It's got to be about money, hasn't it? Do you remember what Stan said – love or money, they're the main reasons why people get killed. And I can't see how love could be involved with Ollie and Mrs F. Ms Zheng's threatening message certainly didn't sound like she was referring to a romance.'

'So what do we do now? It's going to be hard to find out more. We've burned our bridges at the hockey club, thanks to Lydia's gran turning up at the wrong moment. And for all we know the police are on their way out here. But we can't hide in these trees forever . . .'

'We don't have much time,' said Daniel. 'So, we need to take action. The sensible thing to do is find the police, tell them what we've found out and hope they take it seriously. We could take that notebook and the bank statements too? They must be able to figure out the connections. At the very least they need to speak to Mrs Fustemann about her link to the hockey club, and ask Ms Zheng why she was snooping around there.'

'They won't take it seriously, though, will they. They already knew most of this stuff, and don't reckon it's important. They think Lois did it.'

And they're probably correct, despite all this information we're collecting.

Daniel sighed. 'You might be right, and I doubt they would just let us off with another warning, if there's a chance we've got it wrong. We need absolute proof.'

We sat in silence for a minute. I split my twig down the middle and gazed at the clean yellowy woodgrain inside.

'You know what?' Daniel said. 'I haven't got a lot left to lose right now. I'm going to the hospital to see if Mrs Fustemann is awake. She could tell us the whole story, I'm sure of it, whether it was

Ms Zheng or someone else who pushed her down the stairs.'

I stared at him. 'How the hell do you think you're going to get in? They don't let scruffy, bug-eyed kids into their tidy wards. Especially when they're not related to anyone.'

'Are you not coming, then?' Daniel's gaze was as puppyish as I'd ever seen it. 'I thought – we're the last men standing. From the team, you know?'

Heckin' team. Look what it had got me into.

I was really conflicted. I needed to stick with my plan, but I just wasn't *feeling* it right then. Backing Daniel up would only prolong his agony, especially as I knew he was going to end up learning an unwelcome truth. I wished Lois Baynton was the person Daniel thought she was.

'I dunno,' I said. 'Can't you imagine what the police or Mr Scouter are going to say to us already? Skipping school and running around Hanbridge when we've already got detention over it?'

'But – this could be our only chance to find out the truth and save Lois!'

I couldn't stop my face. It pulled into an expression I couldn't control, like a big old *I doubt it* sketched on with felt tip.

Daniel's gaze dropped.

'You don't believe she's innocent, do you?' He was all ice now. '*You* think she did it. And I'm just fooling myself because I'm worried about Mum.' He got up and brushed crumbled leaves off his trousers.

'Well, it's not impossible, is it? The evidence is right in front of you, Daniel. She had means – she's physically very strong; motive – she was hopping mad with her husband for getting into so much money trouble; and opportunity – I saw an ad in the *Gazette* for Lois's yoga classes at Hanbridge High, so she had an access pass to get into school. She could have sneaked in past Mrs Fustemann, maybe once the governors started arriving. It's a no-brainer.'

Daniel shook his head hard. 'What about all the other clues we've uncovered? The debt, the gambling, the threats Ms Zheng made, the fight Baynton was having with Mrs Fustemann . . . and oh, yeah, Lois wasn't there when Mrs F fell down the stairs! I know her, unlike you. *I* know she's not a killer.'

He was getting annoying now. I tried to hold down my temper. 'But, Daniel – all this . . . You've got to see that the police have a huge advantage over us as detectives. I mean, I admit it's been worth it to get my parents all wound up, but when it comes to really finding a killer, there's no way –'

'Wait,' Daniel interrupted. His face was pinched and pale. 'So you never believed me? You were only helping me to make your parents angry! Why?'

I didn't answer straight away. I tried to think of a way to make it sound heroic, but suddenly Plan B felt a bit heartless. 'I didn't want to come to Hanbridge,' I replied eventually. 'I thought me getting into trouble might make them change their minds about this place, move us back to Grensham.'

Saying it out loud made me squirm.

'Oh! That's really nice. And you used me and my mum to do it?'

'No, Daniel. Obviously I wanted to help you –'

'I don't need your sort of help, you . . . *Romulan*[27]. I trusted you! Like an idiot.' Daniel's eyes were accusing, his voice shaking with anger. 'I won't make the same mistake again. If you care more about your own pathetic problems than *real-life* ones, like solving a murder and stopping me getting

27 A species related to the Vulcans, the Romulans have a reputation in *Star Trek* as two-faced, double-dealing and untrustworthy.

taken away by social services, then fine. I'll go to the hospital on my own, and you can go back to school and pretend you're invisible again. *Mak'dar!*'

Ouch. I was all boiled up on the inside. No one told me off like that.

'I'm not a flaming *mak'dar*, whatever that is. I'm just thinking straight – one of us needs to! I don't need you, Daniel, *you* were the one who begged *me* for help. So off you go, and good luck getting into the ward. You'll be squished like a fly before you can get anywhere near Mrs Fustemann.'

Daniel didn't look back as he stomped through the undergrowth. I sat on the little mound of dirt and flumped back into the thin scattering of disintegrating leaves.

I did not feel good.

33

Friday 16 May, 10.35 a.m.

Woodland near the river, Hanbridge

After a couple of minutes of wallowing, I got up and stretched my legs. Without Lydia and Daniel, I felt a bit flat and aimless – what should I do now?

Maybe I could run back to school. No one paid any attention to me there anyway, so perhaps I could sneak into class without anyone realizing I'd gone. That sounded like a good plan. Sure, being chased by Valda Campbell had pushed me a bit further than my usual warm-up did, but that row with Daniel had built up some kind of energy. Everything was tense from my ears to my knees.

Trying to use exercise to shake off the heavy, guilty feeling in my gut, I set off in what I thought was the right direction, back towards school. But jogging that way only got me as far as a garden fence of overlapping wooden planks, all covered in dying leaves and a weird green musty-smelling powder. I followed the fence to the right and pretty soon ended up next to the river, dark and curdled like boiling gravy, a thin grey, unfriendly path following its meandering shape.

I needed to get back to the *road*, not the river. I cursed myself for not paying attention to which way Daniel went when he stomped off. The path seemed to lead back into the trees behind me, not the way I'd come along the fence. So I decided to follow it, the heavy feeling in my stomach starting to churn. No one knew where I was, except Daniel. Before long I'd run back into the wood again.

It was funny how quickly I was completely lost. Civilization was only a few metres away, but in that dense green place I could have been in another world. It felt a bit claustrophobic, the trees bearing down on me, adding to my nerves. I started to breathe faster, feeling shaky, trying to pluck a Boomerangs song from my memory to calm me back down. My thoughts were hurtling into overdrive, and I found myself thinking about Lois stuck in a prison cell, and Daniel's mum, and how she might feel if he did get moved by social services to a Dumping Ground.

That wasn't my business, and I tried to shake it off as I kept jogging, starting to hear passing cars nearby. But the feeling of shame clung to me. Had it really been that mean, using Daniel and Lydia to get back to my old friends? I couldn't help wondering. And what was a *mak'dar*,[28] anyway? I could only think of horrible things it might be. Like a backstabber. Or a selfish pig.

I hurried towards the road sound, but with all the distractions in my brain I forgot to watch my step. Before I could stop, I slipped and stumbled down a steep bank, and crashed into a patch of brambles at the side of the road just as a minivan zoomed past at forty miles per hour.

It missed me, but only just.

I sat down hard on the scruffy verge, skin scratched from the prickles and my pulse beating fast. I could feel tears forming, and I flinched like crazy as my phone beeped several times.

There were three missed calls and a voicemail from Mum. I guessed that there'd been no signal

28 According to Daniel, *mak'dar* is a Klingon insult without an exact translation, but he intended it to mean 'pathetic traitor'. Ouch.

while I was down by the river. I took some deep but shaky breaths and looked around. I was further from school, on the road to the hospital.

Things couldn't get much worse, so I might as well see what the word from Mum was. I dialled voicemail and waited for the new message.

It was pretty bad.

'*Jonathan,* wo bist du?? *I just heard a message from* Schule *that you are not there. I can* NOT *believe you would like this* sich verhalten. *I know you are angry because of the move but this is just cruel, Jonathan. I did not think you were so* unbarmherzig. *You were always so sensitive to other people's* Gefühle! *Call me back* sofort, bitte. *Right now.*'

I probably should have called her back, and put her mind at rest, but what she'd said made me realize there was something I needed to do first.

I *am* sensitive to other people's feelings, and I was feeling terrible because I had been cruel. Daniel had really trusted me, and Lydia ... well, Lydia would probably *love* to know she'd been right, but maybe she did have a point. I hadn't wanted to admit it, but I'd enjoyed being a part of something with them.

In the far distance, I could see Daniel's blonde head along the road. Hospitals are funny places.

Visiting hours, corridors full of trolleys, nurses with too much to do and no patience left – I knew a bit about them after Nanna spent her last few weeks there. He didn't stand a chance.

Daniel needed me, if he was going to get through all that. He didn't deserve to be abandoned, even if his crusade was completely wrong-headed.

And, frankly, I didn't fancy the alternative. Apologizing to Mum, that was going to happen either way. Sucking up to Mr Scouter, hoping he'd put our behaviour down to intense post-traumatic stress? Maybe Monday was soon enough for that.

I sent Mum a text, very short, just saying I was safe and not to worry. Then I turned off my phone and ran.

Daniel must've heard me coming, but he didn't turn round. I stepped along beside him for a couple of minutes, while I got my breath back. He refused to look at me.

So I started walking backwards, right in front of him.

'What are you doing, Jonathan?' he growled. 'I thought you were giving up. Letting the police do things their own way. Abandoning the team.'

'Ah, give me a break. I'm here now.' I hated apologizing.

'What's changed, though? You still think I'm an idiot and wrong about Lois. You always have! Your face when you came to my house – did you not think I'd noticed? How much you were weirded out by me and Mum?'

I went cold. I hadn't thought I'd been as obvious as that.

'I liked your mum –' I started.

'For a minute I thought you might be different from the others. The ones like Tyler who laugh about how sad they think I am. But you aren't, are you? You're only interested in what you can get out of this, and you'll be off at warp nine[29] as soon as you get your own selfish way. Just go back to school, Jonathan, and leave me alone.'

He sounded like he meant it. I stopped on the road. I actually felt really bad. Because he was right about most of it, and I thought he hadn't noticed.

So I sucked it up. Burning in the face, I just said

29 This is as fast as you can go in a starship without getting mutated into a lizard-like protohuman. Sometimes it feels like Dad drives at warp 9.

it once, and I wasn't even sure if he could hear me, but I needed to say it anyway.

'I'm sorry.' I stared down as I scuffed my shoe on the road. 'You're right. I was a rat. A Romulan. Probably even a *mak'dar*. But I'm not using you now. I'm here to help. I promise.'

I heard him take a really deep breath so I closed my eyes, waiting for more yelling.

'Jonathan . . .'

I looked up.

'Oh, come on, then,' Daniel said. 'I suppose we might as well see it through together, seeing as you're here and all.'

'Yeah! We might as well.'

We were both grinning like lemons, but on paper it looked like we both played it pretty cool.

Friday 16 May, 11.20 a.m.

Between Hanbridge and Kingham

The hospital was twenty minutes further down the road, on the edge of Kingham. It was huge, a big old mishmash of knackered and new buildings, all linked with ugly glass corridors. There were blue signs on every corner saying stuff like ACUTE MEDICAL, X-RAY, OUTPATIENTS. Nanna Rosie had been in the Cabot Ward.

'Where do you reckon Mrs Fustemann might be?' Daniel asked.

'We could try intensive care? She looked pretty bad on Wednesday.'

'Would they let us visit, though, in intensive care?

Maybe we should ask someone. We should have brought flowers.'

'I've got four quid. We could go to the shop, and get some chocolate, maybe? Then go to reception and say we've been sent by school.'

'Yeah, like school's going to send a couple of scruffs who look like they've been dragged through a hedge backwards!'

Daniel had a point. We were not really in a fit state after the running and the brambles and the mud and the nettles.

'True. Let's find the bogs, tidy up and go to the shop. Then we can look for an information desk.'

I was hoping we would find a cheap deal in the shop, because my stomach was starting to rumble. I hadn't brought a sandwich, today being school-dinner day, and the four quid was my dinner money. But the cheapest box of chocolates was £3.99, so I had to suffer.

The shop was full of weird mixed-up stuff – balloons and teddy bears and toothbrushes and crossword books. Daniel poked around in the magazines looking for *SciFi Monthly* while I paid for the Milk Tray.

It took us forever to find the right place to ask. The general information desk turned out to be halfway up one of the tower blocks next to a sad-looking cafe filled with sad-looking people. There were three members of staff at the desk and a queue of people waiting to ask them things. Gowned people pushed drip stands along the corridor and flashes of blue scrubs darted in and out of doorways. It was loud, lots of conversations constantly interrupted by beeps and the whirr of machinery in the background.

We waited in the queue, shuffling forward at a slug's pace. The chocolate box felt damp in my clammy hands and I had an itch under my left foot.

Finally it was our turn.

'Hello. Would you be able to tell –'

'We are looking for our great-aunt, Mrs Fustemann –'

Daniel and I both stopped. I'd assumed he'd want me to do the talking, but there he was chirping up with a good cover story. I let him continue.

'Could you tell us where she is?' he asked simply.

The man behind the counter frowned. 'First name? And how you spelling that?'

'Millie, Millie Fustemann. F-u-s-t . . .'

It took him just a moment to check his computer. 'Your auntie's on Ward 5C. That's in the Brunel Building, see.' He whipped out a map and pointed to a spot in the top corner.

'You are here at the moment,' he said, pointing bottom left. 'So you need to go along here, get the lift down, and past the Dietetic Centre . . .'

I couldn't follow it, but Daniel seemed to be listening. We nodded and said thank you and turned to go.

'You do have an adult with you? No children allowed on the wards without adult supervision.'

Hell.

'Oh, yes! Mum's just over there,' Daniel said, waving towards the cafe where a middle-aged woman in a bobble hat was choosing her sandwich from the display.

'*Quick thinking*,' I whispered as we moved out of earshot.

'It's this way,' Daniel said, trying to pretend he wasn't pleased.

We traced the map as we went, moving from left to right in the corridors to avoid being run over by wheelchairs and trolleys. It stank, mostly of disinfectant but also of some kind of disease-y smell.

Finally, we stood outside a door painted light green, like everything else in the world of hospital. We peeked in and saw another desk, staffed by a couple of nurses who were busy writing things down on clipboards.

We pushed through the door. By now my whole body felt itchy. I could feel my heart pumping and my upper lip had gone all sweaty again.

'Hi,' I said in a squeaky voice. I needed to pull myself together. 'We're here to visit Mrs Fustemann. Our headteacher sent us.'

Nurse number one barely looked up. 'Visiting hours are two till four, then six till eight.'

'Would it be OK to just pop in? We are on a free period and we need to get back before French starts ...' Daniel's voice must have revealed his desperation. The nurse looked up from his paperwork at last. He took in Daniel's puppy-dog expression, as I displayed our box of chocolates and smiled winningly, doing my best Lydia Strong impression.

It worked like a charm.

'Well, she *is* in a private room now, so I suppose you wouldn't be disturbing the other patients. Just five minutes, then.' He pointed to a door on the left, past a row of curtains. 'She's on strong painkillers, so you might not get much response.'

Mrs Fustemann was in a metal bed, propped up on a pile of pillows. She was hooked up to a bunch of machines, and her face had come out in all different colours. Her room had a huge window with another (violently pink) curtain across it, and on the bedside cabinet stood a vase of flowers next to a small framed photo of the *Corrie* cast. One of her arms was in plaster. She was asleep.

'I'm not sure I want to wake her up ...' I murmured. Seeing her all weak and damaged didn't make her any less terrifying. She was still The Dragon, after all.

'No choice,' Daniel said. He had this look in his eye, like he'd seen strange new worlds, and I took a bit of courage from that.

He touched Mrs Fustemann's shoulder. 'Mrs Fustemann?' he said quietly.

She moved her head and made a mumbling sound with her dry lips. Her eyes stayed shut.

Daniel repeated himself, with a harder shoulder jiggle. *Not* the one in plaster, I should add.

Mrs Fustemann's eyes cracked open.

'Oozat?' she said in a growly voice. Her good arm came up and she scratched her nose.

'It's us, Mrs Fustemann. Daniel Horsefell and Jonathan Archer. We've come to visit you . . . To ask a few things.'

'Be at . . . school?' she said, only really a quarter with us.

'No, we are at the hospital. You had – you fell . . .' I said, encouraged by her semi-conscious state to speak up.

Mrs Fustemann's eyes flickered. We saw the bloodshot whites of her eyes as they swivelled towards us.

'*Not . . . fall . . . push . . .*' she whispered. Her eyelids quivered.

'Did she just say she was pushed?' I asked Daniel.

He nodded, lips pressed thin.

'Wow.' Lydia's second-victim theory was right after all. My mind was suddenly all awhirl. Lois hadn't been in school that day – she'd been under arrest. So it *wasn't* her. But who could it have been? Who was there at the time?

Who shoved Mrs Fustemann down the stairs?

'Do you know who pushed you? Was it the person who killed Mr Baynton?' Daniel blurted out.

253

Mrs Fustemann kind of shivered. Her eyes shut up tight, and she started to roll her head from side to side across the pillow fretfully.

'No ...' She sounded like a little girl, weirdly. Her fingers picked at the blanket.

I had a flash of inspiration. 'Now come on, Millie, tell us the truth. Who attacked Mr Baynton?' I put as much of Lydia's gran into my voice as possible.

'Mother said ... keep safe ...' Mrs Fustemann seemed really distressed; her face puckered up as if she was going to cry.

'Keep what safe?' I raised my eyebrows at Daniel.

He shrugged. 'Keep going,' he said to me.

'Mother wouldn't want you to lie, Millie. Now just tell us, please, what you know about what happened to Mr Baynton.' I remembered something I'd wondered about. 'Where did you get his whistle from?'

I was starting to feel bad, pestering her like this, but we almost had it.

'Felicity ... didn't mean it. He was bad. I ... I'm a good girl, Mother, I did my best, just like I promised ...' Mrs Fustemann began to sob.

'I think she's covering for her sister!' I grabbed Daniel's arm. 'There's got to be a connection between

Mrs Fustemann's sister and Mr Baynton. She could be the one who killed him and took the whistle!'

'But we don't know *who* her sister is, do we?' Daniel was wide-eyed, staring at Mrs Fustemann's crumpled face. 'That must be what Miss Campbell was about to tell us, back at the hockey club when Lydia's gran turned up. Pox!'

Mrs Fustemann's tears were rolling on to the bright white NHS pillow. I felt awful for pushing her to this point – but there was no one else to ask now. Our only remaining suspect was Ms Zheng, and she certainly wasn't Miss Fustemann's sister, or Miss Campbell would have said.

I bit my lip and leaned over the bed again. 'Tell me about your sister?' I asked more gently.

Mrs Fustemann gargled horribly. I grabbed a tissue from the bedside cabinet and shoved it into her good hand.

'Go on,' I said.

'I had . . . to make sure she didn't get in trouble. Not easy . . . Drawn to the bad ones. And now – it's gone too far . . . Murder! Mother, I couldn't stop it . . .'

Mrs Fustemann was really honking into the tissue now. Daniel touched my shoulder and we moved to the far corner of the room.

'We've really upset her,' Daniel said, all lower lip.

'I know. But it's got to be the answer! We can get the police to look up who Mrs Fustemann's sister is, and they can question her about what she was doing on Monday night. It's a proper break in the case, they can't ignore it.'

'They might be quite unhappy about us plaguing Mrs Fustemann with all these questions while she's so sick, though.' Daniel crinkled up his brow. 'I wouldn't do it to Mum – and Mrs Fustemann isn't even *used* to pain and medicine and that.'

I sighed. He was right. The police might see Mrs Fustemann's confession as complete nonsense because she was on such strong medication. We needed some proof, something obvious that we could take to show DS Norman. I looked back at the bedside cabinet.

'What if she's got a phone? Felicity will be in her contacts – or there might be a picture in her handbag or something? We should have a look.'

I felt a kind of fire burning in my chest; we were *so close*.

Daniel looked a bit sick, but he nodded. I went over and opened the cupboard door. Inside was a large navy handbag, an open packet of plastic gloves and some wadded-up tissue.

I pulled out the bag, carefully grasping it by the handle with the tissue. I didn't want to leave fingerprints all over it, even though I was planning on taking any evidence straight to the police.

Daniel hung back as I put the bag on the end of the bed and nudged it open with my elbow.

'Are you sure about this?' His eyes were fixed on Mrs Fustemann's tear-stained face. She had stopped mumbling and drifted back to dreamland.

'Yes! We can't stop now.' I was still filled with a kind of burning zing. I knew I was going to solve this blasted case and find out who killed Mr Baynton. Not the police, not Lydia, not even Daniel – me.

I grabbed a couple of gloves from the cupboard. They'd do the job better than elbows. I felt like all the SOCOs on all the cop shows, picking my way through Mrs Fustemann's make-up and Polo mints. There was no phone, but she had a big fat purse, red leather with a gold zip and a foldout card section.

I felt my insides roar as I opened the first compartment, cheering me on rather than complaining about its extreme emptiness.

The zip section had two pound coins and an old bus ticket in it. I checked it but the date was weeks ago.

I turned the purse over and snapped the popper. As I unfolded the leather, stuffed with plastic store cards and bank cards, I breathed out in a rush. There was a picture. Two teen girls, a bit fuzzy like old photos are, both of them gawky and grinning with hockey sticks resting against their shoulders.

'Look!' I held it up so Daniel could see.

'I think that's Mrs Fustemann,' he said after an unwilling glance. He pointed to the girl on the left.

'You're right! So this must be her sister. She looks familiar – where have I seen her before?' I searched my mind. I'd only been in Hanbridge a few weeks; it couldn't be too hard.

'You're right. I know that face. She's wearing glasses, but she might have contact lenses now . . .' Daniel was concentrating, his frown pushed right up to the purse.

A voice cut across the steady beat of the machines monitoring Mrs Fustemann.

'Laser eye surgery, actually.'

My whole body froze.

35

Friday 16 May, 12.05 p.m.

Kingham Hospital

A figure stood framed in the gap between the curtains and the closing door.

'Fancy finding you two here,' said Mrs Scouter.

She pushed the door to with a soft click.

'I'd *love* to know why you're going through my sister's bag. You do know that's a criminal offence, don't you? Perhaps I'd better report this.'

My jaw was slack. Mrs Scouter was Mrs Fustemann's little sister? Daniel blew out a loud puff of air, as dumbstruck as I was.

Mrs Scouter seemed to sense our fear. She turned again and snapped the lock on the door. 'Maybe we should have a little chat before I decide what to do with you.'

Ants were crawling around inside my guts and my skin was prickling under my sweaty school shirt. A quick side-eye look at Daniel convinced me that he felt the same.

I put down Mrs Fustemann's purse and backed away from the bed.

'We just came to see if – how Mrs Fustemann was doing. We'll get back to school now, before lunch hour is over . . .'

Mrs Scouter laughed. It wasn't a nice sound.

'Oh, I don't think so. I think you're going to take a few minutes to tell me what you're looking for in that purse. Is it money? Are you genuinely stealing from a sick woman?' Her voice was amused.

'We're not thieves,' Daniel stuttered, unable to take his eyes off her mocking expression.

'I know that,' she spat. 'And I know you lot were poking round again, asking questions. I had a call from Valda at the club, about kids in Hanbridge uniforms snooping round.'

So Mrs Scouter and Mrs Fustemann *were* the Collins sisters Valda Campbell had told us about!

'We weren't doing anything wrong – just asking

about the junior trials at the weekend . . .' I was still sure she knew exactly what we were doing, but it was worth a shot. I'd try anything to get us out of that room.

'Ha! A likely story. I remember you two. You were the ones who found Ollie Baynton's body.' Her voice had gone dangerously quiet. 'And you're still sticking your noses in where they don't belong.' She took a step towards us. 'Give me your phones.'

'N–no, we're not being nosy. We're just concerned about Mrs Fustemann, that's all,' I said.

Daniel was almost jerking, shaking in his socks. I felt it too, the feeling like anything could happen. If Mrs Fustemann had been protecting her sister, that meant Mrs Scouter was the actual killer – and I couldn't see her letting us go.

She was between us and the door. I sneaked a look behind me at the large window, open about half a hand's width to let the breeze in. There were metal rails outside, part of a fire escape. There must be a platform, like a mini balcony, with ladders going down to the ground.

My mind worked nervously. If I could get out, it would leave Daniel locked in a room with a possible killer. But he was braver than me in a lot of ways.

And I'd be able to raise the alarm – get help. I still didn't have any evidence, but if you make a 999 call, they have to take it seriously, right?

I took the chance, starting to sidle slowly backwards, but she caught the movement at once.

'Stay there, boy,' she growled.

'See ya!' I said, and made for the window, scrabbling with the pink curtain. I pushed at the open pane as hard as I could, sensing Mrs Scouter's sudden presence behind me.

'Ow!' Daniel squealed as she pushed past him. He lunged, grabbed and pinched at her shoulder, but he was thrown off like a rag doll. Hands grasped for my back as I leaped up to the knee-high window ledge.

'No, you don't!'

I felt her grab my ankle. I fought, kicking with my other foot, hands braced against the open window frame, gasping desperate breaths as fear crushed my chest.

But she was bloody strong. She pulled hard, once, and I flew feet-first back into the room. My forehead hit the windowsill, and everything went black.

36

Friday 16 May, 12.50 p.m.

Kingham Hospital

My head was a bucket of fire. I unpeeled my dry tongue from the roof of my mouth, which was like sandpaper and tasted of metal.

People in films always act like waking up from a head injury is this confusing hazy crazy experience where they don't know where they are or what's going on. This was not true in my case. I knew I was hurt. I knew I was on the floor, and that my hands and feet were tied tight with something that was cutting into my skin. I knew Daniel was beside me, his back pressed into my arm. I knew I didn't want to open my eyes and see how dire the situation was.

I could hear it was pretty bad, because Daniel was crying. Not sobbing and wailing like Max in a paddy, just kind of hiccuping quietly, like he'd cried himself out already. I wondered how long I'd been unconscious. I wondered where Mrs Scouter was.

I opened one eye, reluctantly. We were in a corner of the room, bundled under the sink, and Mrs Scouter had gone. Mrs Fustemann was still asleep on the bed to my right.

I opened my other eye and nudged Daniel. 'What's going on?'

'Oh, thank God you're awake! I thought you might be . . . you hit that windowsill so hard – and Mrs Scouter is completely mad, she's spitting with rage. I tried to stop her with the Vulcan nerve pinch[30] but it didn't work. I don't know what she's going to do, Jonathan; she said she'd cut my finger off if I made a sound, and I've got a really bad feeling . . .'

'OK, OK. Keep your cool, there's got to be a way out of this mess.' His panic made me want to pretend things were better than they actually were.

30 This is what the non-violent Vulcans use to knock people out in *Star Trek*. Daniel knows it's not for real, but he wasn't thinking too clearly at that moment.

I pulled at the bindings round my wrists. They felt like thin rope and were tied tight and strong. 'Can you undo these strings? With your Paul-whatsit magic skills?' I asked.

'I haven't practised rope! I've been focusing on the handcuffs. I know the theory, but it's precision stuff ... I'm just not skilful enough!' There was still a strangled sob in his voice. 'Mrs Scouter killed Mr Baynton. She must have. What if we're next?'

'She can't kill us in cold blood,' I replied, but a niggle of doubt was working its way into my buzzing head.

Before we could say any more the door opened and Mrs Scouter slipped back in with a cup of hot coffee in one hand. She relocked the door and came over to our corner.

I pretended to be unconscious – not because I was afraid, I just didn't want to look at her horrible face again.

She kicked me in the leg.

'Come on, boy – I want to talk to you.'

I didn't move.

She bent over and pinched my ear like a crab – long, pointy nails digging into my flesh.

'Yow!' I struggled away as best I could. What a witch.

'Aha! I thought you were faking it. Now, tell me what you know and who you've spoken to.' Her voice was tense. She put down the coffee on Mrs Fustemann's cabinet and loomed over me, sharp creased trousers just centimetres from my nose. Instead of the poised and elegant accountant I had seen at school, here was an ogre, a she-devil.

'We don't know anything.' My voice cracked as I tried to sound convincing.

Daniel just cried.

'You wouldn't be here looking through Millie's bag if you knew nothing. Now talk, or shall I give you *both* something to cry about?'

She crouched down beside us, and her hand shot out, talons tugging a chunk of hair on the bruised part of my head. It *killed*.

'Oow ow oww.' My response was too loud for her liking. I couldn't control it; my heart was beating in my throat and my brain had stopped working. Surely a nurse would be in to check on us soon?

'*Enough of the hysterics*,' she hissed. 'Talk.' Mrs Scouter stood back up and folded her arms, muscly beneath her frilly grey blouse, and I remembered the dark bruises round Mr Baynton's neck. Had her hands made those?

'OK – I'll tell you what we know!'

She walked over to the bed and sat beside her sister's sleeping body.

'We know you had connections with Mr Baynton and the hockey club, as well as school. We know Mrs Fustemann and Mr Baynton had arguments.'

'We can see you're violent,' Daniel added.

I forced my brain to think through all the clues we'd come across. The list of numbers in Mr Baynton's notebook floated in front of my eyes and I suddenly remembered one of Mr Sloth's more unconventional maths lessons.

'He was a gambler,' I said quietly. 'You're an accountant. Was that it?'

Mrs Scouter chuckled and clapped her hands, one, two, three.

'Good thinking, boy. It's almost a shame that you'll never get to take a single GCSE.'

She gazed down at us with narrowed eyes. 'I'm a well-respected member of this community. I help out everywhere – the school, the hockey club – I even stood as treasurer of the mayoral committee last year. Everyone is *very* grateful for my help. So few organizations can find *financially* minded volunteers these days.'

Her voice was mocking, and I realized, with a jolt in my stomach, what she was doing. She was explaining her crime, which meant she knew she was going to get away with it, because we were never going to escape.

'It just didn't seem right that I should give so much; devote my life to balancing everyone else's books, and get nothing in return. Do you know how little my husband earns? And how much those *boring* do-gooders raise every year?'

She examined her nails. 'I only wanted a tiny bit back, for some of life's absolute necessities. Three holidays a year, one skiing and two in the sun, plus my Mercedes and the chance to retire early to Monaco –'

'What are you going to do to us?' I interrupted her.

'Look, I don't enjoy this.' She flashed me a twisted grin that suggested otherwise. 'But you can't be allowed to go around spilling the things you've found out. Don't worry, I'm not a monster – I won't torture you or anything.'

I was going to wee myself.

37

Friday 16 May, 12.55 p.m.

Kingham Hospital

'It has to look like an accident. Poor Millie, I shall miss her. But she won't know a thing about it.'

'You – you're going to wipe out *all three* of us?' I tried to pull my legs up in front of me, in a weird self-defence move.

'It's just a shame Ms Zheng isn't here too! She's been making a nuisance of herself as well, poking around in my and Baynton's business. Well, three birds, one stone is efficient enough for now. But before you go – you must want the satisfaction of knowing what it was all about?'

'I've already worked it out,' Daniel said from behind me.

'I doubt that.' Mrs Scouter looked slightly offended.

'But I have. I've been watching *Deep Space Nine* this week, specifically, season two, episode eight. A Bajoran man was hoarding info so he could use it to blackmail others. Someone killed him to stop him spilling the beans on them. And I reckon that's what you did too.' I felt Daniel's head turn as he looked up at Mrs Scouter. 'We started out thinking Mrs Fustemann was involved. And she was, in a way. *You* got her involved, because she made a promise to your mother to look after you and keep you out of trouble. That's kept her pretty busy all these years, I reckon.'

Mrs Scouter laughed, short and harsh. 'I've never been able to get rid of the damned fool. Always one step behind me, watching and tutting from the sidelines. I figured she might as well do something useful while she was at it. She makes the perfect alibi – far too respectable to rouse suspicions. A trip to the cinema on Monday night was the least she could do to help, even if it did mean she had to miss an episode of her precious *Corrie*.'

Daniel breathed in and out heavily, like this was taking a lot of energy. I stayed small and quiet, grateful for the time he was buying us. I gave the rope round my arms a gentle tug, hoping it'd miraculously loosened. No good. I tried not to wonder how Dad and Mum would feel when they heard I was dead.

'So you and Mr Baynton had something going on. Some financial deal that was making you lots of money,' Daniel said.

'Not millions, kid, just a nice little profit. The way I prefer to work is little and often. Once you begin depositing large amounts, the bank manager starts to notice.'

I closed my eyes and conjured up those columns from Mr Baynton's notebook, as best I could remember. The first column was for dates, obviously. I'd already guessed that much. But then – the initials. Could they be . . . sports teams? Like Bristol Town, or Gloucestershire County? I opened my eyes, suddenly certain I was right. The next figure, I supposed, must refer to how much money he'd bet – Mr Sloth had a word for that: 'stakes'. Betting was the thing he'd spent all his borrowed money on. What if Mrs Scouter was supplying some too?

That meant the fraction wasn't a fraction – it was the 'odds' on that result happening. And the final column was the amount of profit they made on their bet. It all made sense.

Date	Teams	Stake	Odds	Profit
2/4	BTVFP	50	3/1	150
3/4	GCVSG	70	7/2	245
10/4	CRVGC	120	9/1	1080
11/4	SLVBC	85	6/1	510

'What was your agreement, then?' I was genuinely curious to know if I was right.

'The deal? Oh, it was a beauty. One of many little local schemes we ran. I just placed a number of small bets on local sports matches, and Ollie Baynton, as referee, made sure we got the right results on the day! Just often enough to win a few thousand here and there. We could have carried on for years . . .'

I gave myself a mental pat on the back. Daniel had probably already known, but I'd figured it out for myself without needing to be told.

'So you fixed the matches. Sounds like you had a decent system figured out. Where did it all go wrong?' Daniel asked.

'Baynton got greedy! He was an ass. I feel a fool for trusting him. His other bets never worked out and his debts were catching up with him, so he thought he'd try a spot of blackmail.'

'He said he'd tell on you if you didn't give him your winnings?' Daniel sounded surprised.

Personally, I thought it sounded exactly like something Mr Baynton would do.

'He threatened to tell the school governors about our deal! He was waving around that stupid newspaper article from the *Hanbridge Gazette*, all about how strange it was that the hockey team lost their match to division two Nailsea. Said he could explain it for them, all right. He had nothing left to lose – the debt collectors were closing in and he'd run out of time to pay them off. Thing was, he didn't just want my money – he wanted to make sure he got the Head of House job too. Thought it would put one over on Ms Zheng.'

So *that* was why he'd been so confident about getting the job!

'Millie here knows all about the side projects – she's become quite the expert in covering up my creative accounting. And she wanted me to pay him! To get rid of him that way. But blackmailers never stop, once they get their teeth into you.'

'Side projects? Local schemes?' I said, struck by the memory of stale fruit shortcakes in the headmaster's office, and Valda Campbell talking about the high cost of running the hockey club. 'You've been nicking money from the school! And all those other places you "volunteer".'

Mrs Scouter looked down at me like I was a squashed snail. 'Well, I thought that was obvious,' she sneered.

'So – you decided to get rid of Mr Baynton another way?' Daniel sounded a bit fainty. His back pressed harder into my shoulder. I took a couple of deep, gulping breaths to try and settle the sicky feeling rising in my throat.

'Like I said, I'm a public figure in this town, and so's my husband. If Ollie had managed to leak this info on me to the press, the scandal would be appalling – we'd lose everything.'

I dared to look up at her again. Her face was a dark dusky red, and she had chewed all her lipstick off. She looked mad, bad and dangerous as hell. She gathered herself together, standing up from the bed and stretching.

'Time is not on my side. I am due at a club luncheon soon, and I need to take care of you lot first.' She turned to hold the end of the bed, looking down at Mrs Fustemann, who was still out cold despite everything that had happened in that small room.

"Sadly, after fifty-six years of protecting my interests, my dear sister has decided that she can no longer keep her solemn promise to our dead mother, and so I can't trust her to keep my secrets. She took my little trophy – you know, Baynton's ridiculous engraved whistle – and threatened me – ME! – with the police!' She tightened her grip on the metal frame.

'I thought I'd fixed her before, but she survived her little trip down the stairs.' Mrs Scouter walked round to a large oxygen canister at the side of the bed.

'Ah, well, boys! When an asset becomes a liability – what can you do? It's just business.'

And with that, she yanked the lever to 'on'.

38

Friday 16 May, 1.10 p.m.

Kingham Hospital

'Hospitals are wonderful resources, but, sadly, also underfunded and understaffed. No one will question how a gas leak could happen, or how a stray spark could ignite it.'

She made sure the door was locked, then came and stood over us again. 'Once this room is full of oxygen, everything in it will burn like a firework. The smoke alone will kill you. I suggest you two close your eyes. Maybe say a little prayer if that helps.' She sniggered, eyes shining.

Daniel quivered beside me. 'Oh, Mum . . .' he muttered.

Mrs Scouter picked up her handbag and strolled over to the window I'd failed to climb through.

'I'll give you a count of ten, how about that?'

My ears picked up a hissing noise, growing louder, coming from the canister in the corner. She was really going to do this.

Mrs Scouter moved the chair under the window and climbed up – surprisingly nimble for someone in mega-high heels.

I started to struggle with my ropes, fiercely this time. Daniel rolled over away from the sink as he did the same.

'Good luck with that, boys. The levels of oxygen in the room should soon be high enough for a little bonfire. I'll count you down! Ten . . . Nine . . .'

I heard the rattle of matches from outside the window. She'd left the blinds half closed but I could make out her shape.

'Eight . . .'

Daniel had stopped struggling. He lay still.

'Don't give up!' I panted.

'It's over, Jonathan. I messed it up. We shouldn't have come to the hospital – I'm sorry . . .'

'Seven . . .'

'I came because I wanted to. Look, Daniel, I can't save us. But you can. Think of Paul Daniels – do some magic!'

'Six . . .'

I wrenched my shoulder trying to pull at the bindings round my wrists and ankles, twisting like a trapped wild animal.

'Five . . .'

I hit my head on the radiator behind me and the pain blossomed through my brain once again like an axe wound. Time slowed; my last few moments. I was going to end, here and now, and there was nothing I could do about it. Mum was going to be . . . Oh God, I couldn't think about Mum. All this risk just to get my old life back. Was it worth it? No. I wasn't going to have a life at all.

'Four . . .'

I was never going to see Mum or Dad or Max again. I suddenly knew, without a shadow of a doubt, that they were much more important than my old mates in Grensham. I tried to make a bargain with the universe: *if I can just survive this, I will be a better person*.

'Three . . .'

Was it going to hurt?

'Two . . .'

I was barely aware of the change in pressure as Daniel suddenly bounced up from the ground, his untied rope falling against my neck. My eyes flew open just in time to see him grab a massive steel bowl from under Mrs Fustemann's bed.

'One . . . Zero!'

He leaped, graceful as a gymnast, across the window – just as the lit match came flying between the open curtains.

There was a tiny sizzle as the match fell neatly into the bowl.

'Help! Help! Fire, murder!' Daniel started to yell. A sound, half yelp, half roar came from the fire escape, and the metal steps began to thunder as Mrs Scouter made a break for it.

'Let us out!' I mumbled, still dazed, but fully aware that I was alive. Daniel, my friend Daniel, had somehow saved us all.

39

Friday 16 May, 1.15 p.m.

Kingham Hospital

Daniel didn't end up untying me until after he turned off the oxygen. I thought that was reasonable, to be honest. He unlocked the door, while I was rubbing my sore shoulder with tingling hands, to admit the nurses who were banging to be let in.

Turns out that when you yell, people really do come running to see what's going on. Three nurses ran in and leaned over Mrs Fustemann, checking her pulse and blood pressure and only sparing us a quick glance to make sure we weren't bleeding.

We scrambled over to the window and leaned out over the fire escape. I didn't expect to see much;

Mrs Scouter was bound to have left the area as quickly as possible.

But I was wrong.

I blinked a few times, taking in the reality of the scene, seven storeys below.

Mrs Scouter was still there, now lying on her front on the concrete paving, kicking backwards and struggling against . . .

You'll NEVER guess.

OK, maybe you will.

Lydia was on Mrs Scouter's back, knee into her spine, fighting her attempts to break free, all the while having some kind of argument with her gran. We could hear Gran's high-pitched voice above Mrs Scouter's curses and yells.

'Lydia Alexandra Strong, stop this assault at once! I knew all that taekwondo was going to lead to trouble. I cannot imagine a single scenario in which an attack on this poor woman would be justified!'

To add to the joy of this picture, Bingo was there too, bouncing around with his lead trailing, and barking excitedly in Mrs Scouter's face as though this was the best game he'd ever played.

I nudged Daniel as I noticed security staff closing in round Lydia, ready to release the poor innocent adult from a monstrous attack by a savage delinquent.

'Hold her!' I shouted, before I even knew I was going to.

One of the nurses in the room behind me reached over and grabbed my good shoulder. 'What are you doing! Be quiet, you're disturbing the patient.'

In that moment I gave no monkeys about their opinion.

'Oi! Up here! Hold that woman!' I yelled as loud as I could.

'She tried to kill us!' Daniel bellowed, probably damaging my hearing for life.

We'd done our best. The nurse grabbed us both and steered us out into the ward.

40

Friday 16 May, 2.05 p.m.

Kingham Hospital

It took a while to get out of the hospital, and we didn't leave alone.

The ward sister had called the police, and our old friend DS Norman rolled up, grim as a gargoyle, well unhappy with the mess we'd made.

'What have you lot been up to now!' He marched us straight to the lift, and as we travelled down to the ground floor the two of us stayed quiet. You know what? It's pretty tiring, being whacked on the head and nearly blown up. I was still in a total daze, so when Lydia came flying across the lobby and clutched at my shoulders it took me by surprise.

'Ow.' My arm and head were still too sore for that level of manhandling.

'Oh, shut up. We did it! She's under arrest! They're taking her into custody!'

DS Norman cleared his throat. 'Who? And why?'

'They heard you shouting, so just to be on the safe side, hospital security took Mrs Scouter and me back into their office. Mrs Scouter's gone out of her mind, spitting and swearing bloody revenge. Which made her far more interesting to the police when they finally rolled up.'

'In case you didn't know, DS Norman, Mrs Scouter is our headteacher's wife. Turns out, she was responsible for Mr Baynton's death, and Lois is innocent. As we told you!' Daniel's voice was fearless. He had practically started to glow.

DS Norman's eyebrows almost hit his sharp hairline. 'Stay here, you lot. I better go and get briefed.'

He strode off to speak to the small group of uniformed coppers by the hospital's security office door. Nearby, Lydia's gran was sitting next to a security guard who'd managed to get her a cup of tea from somewhere.

'How did you know? We didn't figure out it was Mrs Scouter until she showed up.' Not that I wasn't glad that Lydia had arrived when she did, but I was fairly confused about how she did it.

'Just my incredible investigative journalism skills, kid. After the incident at the hockey club, Gran took me back to school for a disciplinary meeting. And while I was waiting outside Mr Scouter's door, I heard him on the phone, trying to get through to someone, but they weren't answering. So he totally said, "Felicity, darling, you must please call me back straight away, I have something urgent to discuss with you". And I figured, the only person you call darling is your child or significant life partner, so Felicity must be his wife. And that's the other name Miss Campbell said – Millie and Felicity. So I figured she must be our missing link.'

'Poor Mr Scouter. So then – you went looking for her?' I asked.

'No, you doughnut. I went looking for you two. I hopped on to the first bus to Kingham, cos I figured you'd go to the hospital to try to speak to Mrs Fustemann. Gran was just setting out for a walk with Bingo, and saw the bus go past with me on it. She bunged him in the car and shot after us. They caught up with me outside the main hospital entrance.'

'Where is he?' I asked, realizing Bingo was nowhere to be seen.

'They don't let dogs into hospitals.' Lydia gave me one of her best *duh* looks. 'He's tied up out front with a bowl of water. Actually, I think it might be a bedpan.'

Daniel hiccuped and went bright pink. My brain caught up suddenly.

'Is that what you caught the match in – a bedpan?' His embarrassment told me there was more to tell. 'A – *used* one? Is that why it sizzled and went out? It was full of The Dragon's pee?'

'No spoilers! Besides, I want to hear the rest of Lydia's story first.' Daniel avoided the question, pushing Lydia right back into the centre of our attention, where she wanted to be.

'So I'm running up the path, trying to stay ahead of Gran and Bingo, who's barking because he thinks I want him to play chase, when I look up and see Mrs Scouter scrambling down a fire escape right ahead of me.'

'And you immediately thought, I'll just rugby-tackle her to the ground?' I still couldn't believe Lydia would do that.

'Yep,' she said, folding her arms and lifting her

chin. 'She was swearing a lot and trying to make a quick exit. And I just figured, oh, the boys have found her out, and I didn't want her to get away scot-free, so . . .'

'So you brought her down,' Daniel said, slowly shaking his head in wonder.

'Yeah,' Lydia said.

'You are amazing,' I said, and I meant it. Imagine having the nerve to do that, based on almost no evidence?

'Gran didn't think so. But then you yelled, and the security men heard it, and Mrs Scouter was so obviously ready to punch her way out of the situation that Gran thought she'd better back me up.'

'Why did they decide to arrest her?' I was trying to put the puzzle together.

'She was ridiculously furious, and every time she opened her mouth some lovely new bit of information popped out, like how Ollie Baynton deserved everything he got and that she'd like to wring those boys' necks too. The inspector wrote it all down and cautioned her and that was it, case closed.'

'Wow. I can't believe we did it.' Daniel's face shone like a supernova. I'd only seen him being miserable, or a bit defeated, before now. Happiness turned him into a toothpaste advert. 'Ms Zheng must have figured out that he was fixing the hockey matches he was refereeing outside school – that's what her message meant! She was on the same track as us all the time. I bet she'll have told the police already, and that'll back up our evidence.'

'Oh, yeah. I guess they'll have to release Lois now!' I grinned too, glad to see him so triumphant. It made me feel like the last few days of stress were truly worth it.

'OK, you kids,' said DS Norman as he rejoined us. 'I'm going to take you back to your homes for some food and rest, and your parents will need to bring you down to the station tonight to make full statements. Then we'll decide whether there are any charges to be brought. I can think of a few – maybe possession of an offensive bedpan, or use of unreasonable force while performing a citizen's arrest.' DS Norman's flat tone was difficult to interpret. I just had to hope he was being uncharacteristically hilarious.

DS Norman put his arm through Lydia's gran's and helped her to the squad car. She was in no fit state to drive. She looked like she needed a stronger cup of tea, or possibly a pint of gin.

We all stayed quiet on the way home. I was still aching all over from Mrs Scouter's attacks – you'd have thought they'd at least give me paracetamol at a hospital. Daniel was gazing starry-eyed out of the car window, towards a brighter future.

Friday 16 May, 2.30 p.m.

My house

I wish I could spare myself the memory of what Mum and Dad said when I arrived home in a squad car, starving and injured and, most importantly to them, uneducated.

Mum was beside herself, couldn't decide whether to thump me or cuddle me, but in the end she combined the two into a tight, uncomfortable bear hug.

Dad gave me another of his famous Looks and stepped to DS Norman to talk about what time we needed to be at the police station. Still clutched in Mum's arms, I didn't have the chance to turn and wave before Dad closed the front door and I heard the patrol car move on.

'Jonathan Henry Archer.'

That's never a good start, is it.

'Yes, Dad?'

'Get in the kitchen right now. We need to talk.'

Talk, talk, talk, talk. That's what we did for the next half an hour.

Their faces as they absorbed the information were grey and shocked. There was a moment's stunned silence before they launched into a new round of questioning.

'What would we have done if that terrible woman had succeeded in hurting you?' Dad said.

'When will you learn that your actions can have terrible consequences?' Mum butted in without waiting for me to answer.

'And why did you get yourself into this situation in the first place? It's not like you to get mixed up in things like murder investigations!' Dad capped it with a final, and answerable, enquiry.

I should have been overwhelmed, but Mum didn't stop hugging me the whole time. I looked from Mum's face and over to Dad's at the other end of the table. Max grinned stickily as he chewed on a fruit bar.

'I'm not sure if you noticed,' I started quietly, 'but moving to Hanbridge was exactly the opposite of what I wanted. So I thought if I got in *enough* trouble, and showed you what a rubbish place this is, you might take us back home. Grensham-home.'

Dad's gaze flicked down to the lino. Mum put a hand up to her temples and rubbed them as though she was trying to erase something.

'Hmm,' Dad said. 'Perhaps we could have been a little less gung-ho about the move. More sensitive. Asked your opinion.'

Mum's eyes had a rim of tears. 'Jonathan, I am very sorry for being a pushy person about moving away from your friends. We did not give you warning enough, I can see that now. We assumed, I think, that you would get used quickly to the changes and make new good friends.'

'Well . . .' I paused. Because, actually, I kind of had made some good new friends, hadn't I? 'I'm sorry too. I didn't really expect it to get so dangerous –'

'Do you think these new young people that you are sneaking around with are to blame?' Mum interrupted. 'I wonder really whether Jayden and Kinsey were so bad. Perhaps this was after all a terrible idea. Perhaps we should turn indeed around and go back to Grensham where these awful things do not happen. I do not want to see you all bruised and battered from attacks by headteachers' wives again.'

I opened my mouth, ready to tell her that going back to Grensham was all I really wanted, when I realized I hadn't looked at my phone for hours.

Dad chimed in with his thoughts. 'I hate to say it, Anneka, but you might be right. I'm not sure I like Hanbridge High. It's changed a lot since I was there. We *could* sell this house, and buy something a bit snugger back in our old area?'

I looked at them, both frowning in concentration, and I thought pretty hard about what I was going to say in reply. I thought about what Daniel had done for me today, and how I'd felt looking down the fire escape and seeing Lydia.

'The new friends – Daniel and Lydia – I dunno. They're kind of all right, actually,' I said. 'Do you think . . . Could we . . . give it another chance? See if things improve?'

Dad snorted. 'Well, that's a U-turn bigger than the government! We'll need to think about it and, if we do decide to stay, just bear in mind that we'll be keeping a much closer eye on you from now on, Jonathan. If you ever skip school again, you'll be in a world of trouble.'

But then Dad made me a sandwich, which is one of his specialities. I ate it in three bites, so he made me another – cheese and pickle, sharp and sweet and crunchy. Mum watched me eat it with misty eyes. Then I went upstairs, past Nanna's framed collection of family portraits, and unpacked my guitar. It was horribly out of tune, but the whole process of turning the pegs and picking through the strings calmed me down like nothing else had over the last few weeks. It felt like coming home.

Friday 16 May, 7.20 p.m.

Hanbridge Police Station

Mum ended up taking me down to the police station this time, and made a concerted effort to get me smartened up for the occasion.

'You need to look like a responsible citizen, not a *zerknittert* boy who cares nothing about anything.' She forced me into a school shirt and one of Dad's most boring ties.

Lydia was already waiting in the lobby. An elderly gentleman dressed in beige, chin covered in white stubble, sat beside her with his arm round her shoulders. He had wrinkles in all the right places, showing how much he smiled.

'Is this one of your friends?' he asked, and Lydia nodded.

'This is Jonathan and his mum. Jonathan, this is my gramps.'

I had already deduced this fact, so I crossed my eyes at her while Gramps and Mum exchanged names and handshakes.

'How's your gran?' I asked.

'Gone to bed. Gramps reckons she hasn't had a shock like this since Great-Uncle Roger came home from Borneo with a facelift.'

Daniel didn't turn up till ten past, but it was OK because DS Norman had been round to pick him up. And guess who was with him?

Daniel's mum had put on outdoor clothes – a long grey dress and a duffel coat – and conquered the stairs, the car and a wheelchair ride.

'Hi, Jonathan,' she said. Her face was still pale, but her eyes had a triumphant gleam.

'Hi, Becky! It's so great that you're here. How's Lois?' I asked.

'On her way home. They dropped all charges and we'll be able to see her later.' She reached up from the chair and squeezed my hand. 'Well done, you!'

Mum gave me a nudge. 'And who is this, Jonathan?'

'Becky Horsefell. Daniel's mum.'

'Most pleased to meet you.'

While they started on the dull getting-to-know-you chat, Daniel, Lydia and I crowded into the corner furthest from the reception desk, where DS Norman was getting us all visitor badges. Daniel had the notebook and bank statements, and he'd dressed for the occasion in his full Starfleet uniform. I didn't comment. Why shouldn't he, if he was happy?

'Are we telling them everything, then?' I murmured.

'Probably best.'

'Can I know now?' Lydia broke in. 'What's the deal with this Lois?'

Daniel bit his lip. 'Hmm. I don't want to tell you if you're going to report it in the school paper. Do you promise to keep this fully between us?'

Lydia shrugged. 'Yeah, if you want. I've got enough material to fill two editions already, to be honest. I can let this one slide.' She grinned at us, and Daniel's shoulders relaxed.

'OK, then.' Daniel glanced at me and took a deep breath. 'Lois is Mum's best friend. She helps me keep Mum safe and well. When Lois was in prison? It was a nightmare – Mum kept expecting social services on the doorstep, ready to take me away. She's ill, you see – chronic fatigue syndrome. And she's not getting any better.'

'Wait.' Lydia raised her brows in disbelief. 'Why would they take you away?'

'Because it was just me – looking after Mum. Part of her CFS is bad anxiety, and losing me is her worst nightmare. It's mine too, to be honest. She heard the nurses say something like it, back when she first got ill. And she's so tired from feeling ill that she can't stop herself worrying.'

Lydia's face had this weird expression, something between disappointment and dismay.

'Daniel Horsefell,' she whispered. 'Are you telling me this *whole* investigation has been driven by your mum thinking the SS were on her tail?'

'Well . . . yeah, I guess so. She gets really jittery, and I don't seem to be able to convince her it's all OK.'

'But you don't have to convince her all by yourself! Have you never heard of young carers' groups? Never seen those documentaries where they talk about getting carers extra help from charities?'

'Err – no?' Daniel's eyes opened wide. 'We don't

watch much TV, to be honest – just Netflix and *Star Trek* DVDs . . .'

Lydia folded her arms. 'The whole point of social services is to try and keep families together. They would offer *help*, not split you up, not unless there was no other choice. Five minutes' internet research could have set her mind at rest. And yours too! I bet the school don't even know, do they? You'd get fewer detentions if they knew why you were always late –'

'It's not always that simple, though,' Daniel said, as he curled his fingers into his palms. 'Anyway, how come you're the world expert?'

I thought I knew. 'Bit of personal experience, maybe?' I said.

Lydia's eyes landed on me hard. 'No comment, except that maybe mums aren't always what they're cracked up to be. And sometimes grandparents can be a very decent substitute.'

'So – your mum's not a surf teacher . . .?' Daniel started to try and figure it out, but a nudge from my left foot made him clam up before he went too far. We really didn't need to know the details if Lydia wasn't ready to tell us.

DS Norman opened a door and beckoned us all to follow him down a long corridor.

'Daniel, or should I say Captain Kirk, you're first.' DS Norman ushered Daniel into the interview room, and Mum pushed Becky's wheelchair in after him.

Mum and Lydia's gramps wandered off to get cups of coffee, while Lydia and I sat together on the hard bench. I took some deep breaths, wondering how Mum would react to my statement about all the dodgy stuff we'd done in the last couple of days. She already knew that we'd hacked Mr Baynton's Facebook, but we'd done a fair bit more since then.

Down the corridor, a room opened up and DI Meek stepped out, in conversation with a short constable carrying a notebook.

'Can't it wait?' she was saying, irritated, heavy footsteps echoing away from us.

'The call is from the Chief Super, ma'am,' her assistant panted, hurrying to keep up.

The door they'd come through hit its frame and swung back open. We could hear the faint sound of someone speaking inside.

'That voice feels familiar,' I said.

Lydia looked at me and listened for a few seconds. 'Yes! It sounds like – assembly . . .'

'Mr Scouter! What's he doing here?'

'Well, his wife has just been charged with murder, so I expect he has to tell them anything he knows and where he was at the time –'

'Shall we listen?' I was suddenly intensely interested. Eavesdropping was kind of my new superpower, after all.

Lydia and I crept along the corridor and peeked into the room. 'Ooh!' she whispered. 'It's got one of those two-way mirrors like on *Brooklyn Nine-Nine*!'

I definitely couldn't resist that.

43

Friday 16 May, 7.25 p.m.

Hanbridge Police Station

Mr Scouter was looking pretty het up when I sneaked into the dark, narrow room, leaving Lydia on guard outside. Through the mirror-wall I could see him sitting opposite a police officer, who had an old-school tape machine whirring on the desk beside him.

'I told you, I'd had a very busy evening and didn't notice what time she came home. Felicity went to the cinema with her sister after the governors' meeting, and when she got in, she seemed completely normal. She's not an actress, she could never have pretended everything was OK if it wasn't.'

'How do you explain, Mr Scouter, her attempt to kill both her own sister and two of your pupils at Kingham Hospital this afternoon? And her admission of this before numerous witnesses?'

Mr Scouter deflated a bit. He took out a handkerchief and blew his nose, dabbing at his cheeks as he considered this. Then he sat up straight and tapped the desk.

'Because she was trying to cover for me. She knows I'd lose everything! My job, my career – and she loves me too much to bear it. So she was trying to make it look like it was all her fault by getting rid of the witnesses . . .'

'Are you trying to say it was *you* who murdered Oliver Baynton, sir?' The interviewer, his back to me, was heavily sarcastic.

'Yes! Yes, I did it, OK? He was blackmailing me, he had written evidence that I was the mastermind behind certain . . . illegal activities that he was involved in. So that night, I met him outside the PE shed and, when he thought I'd handed him the money, I hit him on the head. Really hard. But he wasn't dead, so I had to strangle him with my school lanyard. So you can let Felicity go. She's innocent.'

Lydia hissed at me from the door. 'What's he saying?'

'Shhh!' I needed to hear what came next; so far none of it made sense.

The police officer leaned back towards the mirror and scratched his neck.

'So did you also encourage your wife to try to kill her sister Millicent Fustemann and the two boys, names of . . . Jonathan Archer and Daniel Horsefell?'

'Well, no, like I said, that was her trying to protect me. Shouldn't you be reading me my rights?'

I gazed unbelievingly through the glass. There was no *way* Mr Scouter had killed Mr Baynton! His explanation just wasn't convincing, and for sure he didn't know squat about the crime.

'All in good time, Mr Scouter. First you're going to have to talk me through exactly what happened on the evening of May the twelfth, Monday night.'

Mr Scouter leaned forward and placed his hands flat on the table. I held my breath, waiting for the next bit. It seemed obvious to me that something was seriously wrong.

'Well, when he arrived, it all turned sour pretty quickly. He said he knew what I'd been up to, and that I'd have to pay him off – both by agreeing to give him the Head of House job, and with ten thousand pounds in cash. Of course, I knew what would happen if I paid up. I'd be under his thumb permanently. So I took the opportunity to finish him off; you know, whack him round the head and then . . .' He trailed off.

The police officer cleared his throat slowly. 'And you hit him with – what?'

'A cricket bat.'

.'Right. Thank you, sir. I probably ought to say at this point that you are under arrest on suspicion of murder. You do not have to say anything, but it may harm your defence if you do not mention when questioned something that you later rely on in court. Anything you do say may be given in evidence.'

No way. I was shaking my head. No way did I just see my headteacher get cautioned *on a murder charge*!

'He didn't do it,' I said loudly, eyes fixed on Mr Scouter.

'What happened?' Lydia came in and stood close by me, staring at Mr Scouter.

My head had started to feel heavy.

'Is he under arrest?' she asked.

'Yes! He was trying to get Mrs Scouter off. But then, why would he say ...?' I swayed to the side and realized I could see two of everything.

'Are you OK?' Lydia asked. 'You've gone a bit pasty.'

Once the police officer had finished handcuffing Mr Scouter to a loop on the desk he stood up, and walked quickly out of the door and up the corridor.

And that's when I saw it. Twice, thanks to my woozy eyes. Mr Scouter, alone in the interview room, raised his eyes to the ceiling and smiled.

Not a smile like he'd do in assembly, one to show us what a jolly good chap he was, but, like, a sneaky, sideways sort of smile. It lasted a second or two before it was gone.

And then I was sick on the floor.

44

Friday 16 May, 7.30 p.m.

Hanbridge Police Station

'Jonathan! Lydia! What the hell do you think you're doing in there?'

Caught red-handed, yet again.

I lifted my head to the mirror and saw Mr Scouter sit up taller.

'What a mess! What's the matter with you?' DS Norman made me sit down with my head between my knees and began another lecture about sticking our noses where they weren't wanted.

'Confidential interview . . . No right to observe . . . Hope you realize what a breach of trust . . .' I couldn't really hear what he was saying.

I was staring up at several Lydias and she was staring at me.

Booming around my head was the knowledge that Mr Scouter hadn't been lying. He'd been making mistakes on purpose.

What could I do? I felt woozy and awful, and DS Norman didn't let me get a word in. I reckoned that if he never saw me again it would be too soon. And so, before I knew it, I was out of the station and in Mum's car, on the way back to Kingham Hospital.

The hospital did a bunch of tests. Turns out I had delayed concussion from when I hit my head on the windowsill in Mrs Fustemann's room. The knock had really scrambled my brain. They kept me in overnight for observation and as I lay on the cool, crisp hospital sheets listening to the blips and creaks of the monitors I couldn't stop thinking about that creepy smile.

I hadn't imagined it – Mr Scouter was gloating.

Mr Baynton had finger marks round his neck – I'd seen them – meaning he'd died from manual strangulation. He definitely wasn't throttled with a narrow lanyard, and the police would know by now that there were no cricket bats in the shed.

Was it possible that Mrs Scouter *wasn't* the killer? How could that be, though? She'd said all that stuff, about how he deserved all he got – and she'd been the one placing bets on Mr Baynton's fixed matches.

But if it was all Mr Scouter's idea . . . if they were working *together* . . . either one of them could have done the deed. At the very least she'd been a willing accomplice.

It all kept going through my head like scraps of video, and it took way longer than it should've to get to sleep. But the concussion must've really done a number on me, because I didn't wake up again for fourteen hours.

Saturday 17 May, 11.45 a.m.

Kingham Hospital

That night I had some weird dreams, like trying to play guitar at the Battle of the Bands with no arms, and instead of Kinsey on bass it was Lois Baynton, crying and smiling, and there was a Vulcan on vocals.

When I woke up on Saturday morning, part of my dream had come true. Sitting next to me, holding the biggest bunch of grapes in the world, was Lois, gazing at me with moist eyes. Mum stood at the end of the bed, keeping an eagle's watch over me.

'Mrs Baynton's come to talk to you,' Mum said unnecessarily.

'Hello, Jonathan,' Lois said. 'How are you feeling? Perhaps you aren't really up to visitors yet, but I just needed to say thank you for everything you did for me.'

I shuffled my shoulders up the pillow and pulled up the duvet to cover my pyjamas. I was still half asleep. 'Hi,' I croaked. 'You got out.'

'I did! Thanks to you, and to Daniel of course. And someone called Lydia, who I must also make the effort to visit.'

'No probs,' I said.

'You have made us very proud with helping to clear this nice lady's name' Mum's voice had a little wobble in it.

I reached up to touch the giant bulging bruise on my forehead, which was filling my head with pounding pain.

Mum saw me grimace. 'Hold on, *Liebling*. I'll get a nurse. I expect you need a top-up of paracetamol. It is a *sehr* long time since your last dose.' She went off to the nurses' station.

Lois smiled at me. 'I brought you some grapes – it's not much, but it's traditional. But if you ever – I mean, honestly, if you ever need help with anything. Maybe a free yoga class? Just ask.'

'Thanks. I'll bear that in mind. But we just did what anyone would.'

Mum came back with a stern-looking nurse, who handed me two white pills in a paper cup. I swallowed them down and leaned back against the pillow.

'I'll have to ask you to leave now, Mrs Baynton,' the nurse said. 'Jonathan here needs quiet and rest. Parents only for the rest of the day.'

'Of course. Goodbye, Jonathan. Hope you're feeling better very soon. And thanks again.'

'Bye, then,' I mumbled before my mouth gaped in a huge YAWN. I couldn't keep my eyes open. Back to sleep I went, before Lois had even had a chance to gather up her handbag and leave the room.

Mum came back into the hospital on Sunday morning, grinning like the Cheshire Cat. She'd brought me fresh clothes as well.

'You are coming home, Jonathan! Doctor Green rang us up last evening and said that you were past observing, now, so I have brought your trousers and sweater. And you have had an email, from the Grensham friends, which you will very much like to read.'

I was pleased to be going home (though I'd been enjoying the back-to-back *Murder, She Wrote*[31] episodes on the hospital TV) but alarm bells were ringing all over the shop. 'You've been on my computer?' I asked. 'You can't just go on people's computers without permission, Mum!' I was aware of the irony, after everything Daniel and Lydia and I had been up to, but I mean, talk about invading my privacy.

'Well yes, but only because Kinsey's father texted me yesterday and mentioned they had been expecting for you to reply to some important message! And I was too nosy to wait, *Knuddelbär*.' Mum patted my shoulder and went to find the nurse to sign me off the ward.

I pulled on my least favourite jeans – not sure I could wait, either.

Back at home I switched on my creaky old computer and plugged my phone in to charge it. The battery had died more than twenty-four hours ago, and the number of dings, dongs and buzzes that came through all in a rush made quite the noise.

31 *Murder, She Wrote* is a 1980s American crime drama series featuring nosy mystery writer and amateur detective Jessica Fletcher. Nanna Rosie always said she looked a bit like her, but that was wishful thinking.

HEY look at your DMs, we made you a surprise! — message from Kinsey.

COME ON RAED IT YOU@RE GOING TO BE SO CHUFFED — that one from Jay, who had rubbish typing skills.

And there were more, from nearly all my friends. I had more texts in that one moment than I'd had since I left Grensham.

Finally my PC was ready and I clicked in to my Discord. They'd made a new DM group chat.

New REALM invitation:

Jay_MonsterAA has invited you to join their new

Minecraft Realm, THE OLD HANG OUTS: use this link

realms.gg/6565688_ddr

I clicked the link and *Minecraft* opened up. My knees jiggled against the bottom of my desk as I waited.

And there it was. A spawn room, covered with signs, telling me where to go and what this was.

This is a gift for you Morticia

Everywhere we could think of in Grensham!

We'll be here every Tuesday and Friday 8 p.m. to hang
out/stay in touch ☺☺
We can do quests and if you get the right mod we can
play basketball too
We could play music sometimes too if you wanna jam
We've been working on this all week!!!
Start dead ahead through this door ^^^

I felt a lump in my throat as I scanned around the
online room. It was a masterpiece! First up they'd
built a house. My old house, on my old road. I went
in through the front door, and it looked just the same
(well, as close as you can get with virtual blocks).

I spent the next few minutes exploring the world
they'd built for me. It was completely amazing. The
school was there, the basketball court at the old
recreation park, even the hill we used to slog up on
our bikes for the best view in Oxfordshire. I couldn't
wait till Tuesday, so I messaged the group chat and
one by one they all came online, wanting to know
how I was and what I'd been up to.

'Jonno! How's it going! D'you like it?' Jayden was
first on.

'It's ace! But I thought you'd forgotten me?' I tried to sound jokey.

'NEVER GONNA HAPPEN,' Kinsey chimed in.

'We've been busy setting this up and didn't want to spoil the surprise. Tell us about the murder! And about your new school?'

I didn't log off for hours; we built a bunch of new buildings, just for laughs, though eventually I had to call it quits – my post-concussion headache was absolutely raging.

Mum made toad-in-the-hole for tea, my top favourite dinner of all time, and Max insisted on sitting on my lap to eat his. Apparently, he'd missed me while I was in hospital, which was kind of nice. Dad offered to help me unpack some of the stuff in my bedroom, so it looked like he might be happy to stay, or at least see how things went for a bit.

A good day. But I knew there'd be a tomorrow, and consequences to face.

46

Monday 19 May, 8.25 a.m.

Hanbridge High School

I was sent back to school on Monday morning, of course. Daniel was waiting for me at the gates, still wearing his Starfleet communicator badge. He opened his mouth to speak, but we were interrupted by a gang of Year Nine girls.

'Did you two *actually* get Mrs Scouter arrested?' one of them said, while the others giggled and gawped.

Daniel and I glanced at each other. He shrugged, and smiled his new gigantic smile; I nodded.

'That is EPIC.'

'Amazing.'

'Awesome.'

'Lydia Strong helped too,' I said quickly.

Daniel drew me away, leaving the girls to their gossip. 'You feeling better? We've got to go and see Mr Scouter,' he said.

'Mr Scouter? He's here?' I said, my heart dropping into a beat that was kind of sketchy.

'Yeah. Where else would he be? Lydia's got to come too. She's just putting her food tech stuff in the lockers.'

I floated down the busy corridor behind Daniel, who was clearly still jazzed as heck at being called amazing and awesome. My body felt like it belonged to someone else. I jumped a mile when the registration bell went off, and then again when Lydia pushed through some double doors to our right.

'Morning!' she said, falling into step. 'Just got a pat on the back from Ms Zheng. We seem to be celebrities round here.'

'Hey, stop.'

They looked at me curiously; we huddled into a corner behind some storage shelves.

'I've got news,' I said, keeping an eye out left and right.

'Yeah – I know. Mrs Scouter's been charged and had bail denied. It's great!' Daniel grinned, but it faded as he noticed I wasn't feeling the same joy.

'It's just that –' I started, but Lydia jumped in.

'I think Jonathan may have overheard something on Friday night – at the police station.'

I nodded and took a deep breath. 'I'm not one-hundred-per-cent sure it was all her – Mrs Scouter.'

Daniel blinked. 'Who else could it be? She admitted it – you heard her, Jonathan.'

'She said Mr Baynton *deserved* it, yes. And that he was her partner in the gambling scheme . . .' I squinted, trying to remember exactly what she said.

'Look, we heard her admit she was the killer, at the hospital.'

'Yes, OK. But when Mr Scouter gave his statement he made a load of mistakes on purpose, so they'd realize he was lying and let him go. Think about it. He might actually have been trying to make Mrs Scouter look even *worse*, if she tried to blame it all back on him. He'd already be ruled out by the police, because his story didn't add up. Detective novelists call it a double bluff, when you tell someone the truth badly, so they believe the opposite.'

Lydia looked from Daniel's face to mine. 'So you think Mr Scouter was the mastermind behind Mrs Scouter's criminal ventures?'

'He said Mr Baynton had found out about his illegal activities. That bit could be true. There could be more going on than we know about.'

'You mean – there were other "projects" they were both working on, aside from the gambling and the dodgy accounting?'

We all stared at the floor in an awkward silence.

'I guess we've done what we can,' I said.

Lydia sighed. 'I guess so,' she said. 'We can go our separate ways and get on with our lives now that Mrs Scouter's banged up.'

I was surprised I hadn't thought of that.

'We'd better go and see Mr Scouter, anyway. He's expecting us,' Daniel said. I could see why he wasn't keen that the case might not be over. We'd just got it all sorted, and here I was trying to make it complicated again.

'Come on, then,' I said. We had to walk past the stairs where Mrs Fustemann had fallen. No, that was wrong. Where she'd been *pushed*.

Mr Scouter was waiting for us at his office door. He was not smiling.

'In you come. Remove your *Star Wars* badge, Mr Horsefell; I don't see that on the uniform list.'

He closed the door behind us and it felt like there was a spider crawling down my spine. This wasn't as relaxed as our last meeting. There were no biscuits anywhere.

'Sit down,' he said and gestured to the uncomfortable seats. We lined up in front of him like ducks at the fairground.

'With regard to your unauthorized absence on Friday, you will receive the appropriate disciplinary consequence, which will take the form of five after-school detentions, added to the ten you had already earned through your computer hacking in the PE office. These detentions will then be *doubled*, owing to the seriousness of the misdeeds you have perpetrated. They will begin this afternoon, and you won't be finished until at least half term. I will, of course, notify your primary caregivers.'

All the time he was talking, Mr Scouter was riffling through paperwork at his desk.

Then he raised his head suddenly and I felt Lydia flinch beside me.

'As to the arrest and imprisonment of my wife, I hold no grudges, of course. As the guilty party she, too, must accept the consequences of her actions.'

'But –' I couldn't help it.

'But what?' Mr Scouter's piercing eyes bored into mine, and a tiny muscle in his cheek pulsed.

'I heard that they were looking at other suspects . . .' My mouth had gone drier than the bottom of a budgie cage. I wasn't going to accuse him of anything to his face, let's get real.

'There were others, I believe, who had to be ruled out; but in the end, an eye-witness statement confirmed the case against poor, misguided Felicity. A very difficult decision for dear Mrs Fustemann to make, of course. But what else could she do? Such a loyal soul. And so very distressed to hear that her own sister had made two attempts on her life.'

So Mrs Fustemann had firmly pinned the murder on her sister! I guess it made sense. After all, Mrs Fustemann would lie down in the mud if it meant Mr Scouter could keep his wellies clean.

'Aren't they sisters?' Lydia said, as if she was wondering who Mrs Fustemann would be loyal to.

'They are, yes. But justice must be done,' Mr Scouter said. He smoothed his moustache and twisted his mouth into the same sneaky smile I'd seen before. I felt Daniel go tense on my other side.

'We'd better get to lessons,' I said.

'Of course. And just remember – I will be keeping an eye on you to make sure you stick to the rules of the school from now on. I suggest you use your considerable time in detention to think about the direction you wish to take in life, all of you.' Mr Scouter got up and put out a hand for us to shake. I didn't know how to avoid it without causing offence, so I took it. He squeezed hard.

He opened the door to let us out, and we trudged past Mrs Fustemann's empty desk.

'And do take care of yourselves,' came a sudden call from behind us. His tone of voice suggested he didn't mean it.

I was ice, and my skin felt a size too small.

'I think we might need to be on our best behaviour from now on,' Lydia whispered as we tiptoed carefully towards maths.

47

Monday 19 May, 12.45 p.m.

Hanbridge High School canteen

I was waiting in the canteen queue for lasagne, just minding my own business, though I couldn't help but notice I was the centre of attention once more. Everyone seemed to know about what we'd done. Finn MacKenzie, aka the coolest kid in Year Eleven, had even given me a high five as he passed me along the maths corridor that morning, and I'd had a few proper smiles from the kids in my tutor group.

I was about to get served next when Lydia and Daniel came up out of nowhere. 'We need a word,' Lydia said.

'OK. I'll just get my lunch,' I said.

Lydia nodded and they stood waiting nearby.

The lasagne was dry, and the chips looked under-cooked. I took my tray, turned round and came face to face with Tyler Jenkins, standing in front of a whole gang of other kids.

'What you l-looking at, keeners?' He turned and whispered something to Jerome. The rest of them were looking at us like they were all in on a joke. I guessed we were it.

'Nothing,' I said. I took a step back and trod on Lydia's toe.

'Time for a club m-meeting, is it? Doing a bit more detecting, Mr Poirot and his s-saddo friends? I bet we could come up with some really interesting crimes, innit?'

Daniel sighed. His mouth was pinched. He pushed me gently to one side and stepped up to Tyler. 'Just stop it, Tyler. That's enough. We're not taking it any more.'

'Oh, yeah?' Tyler's expression was disbelieving. 'Who's g-going to stop me?'

'Don't underestimate us,' Daniel said, with a tone to his voice I didn't recognize.

Lydia stepped forward and joined in. 'Too right.

You don't have the nerve to start something in here, Tyler. Not with me, anyway.'

You could hear a pin drop. Everyone was watching.

'Do you remember the last time you tried to pick on me? Back in Year Four? I wedgied you so hard you were singing soprano for a week. And if you think I'm hard, Jonathan here is a black belt fourth dan.'

I expected him to react fiercely. But instead I saw a tiny seed of doubt blossom in his eyes.

I tried to look tough. My turn to speak up. 'You'd best jog on. And take your bunch of back-up dancers with you.'

Then the whole room erupted into cheers and laughter. A few people even clapped. They were with us, against Tyler, and he knew it.

I waited, holding my breath.

'Huh,' Tyler said, embarrassed and uncertain. 'Come on, then. Let's get a football,' he said, and the whole gang trooped off.

Lydia smiled at me. 'And that, my friends, was how you bluff.'

I followed her past the teachers' lunch table to some empty seats. Daniel stuck close behind, grinning to himself.

'Now, Jonathan,' Lydia started as soon as we sat down.

'You can call me Jonno,' I said. 'If you like.'

Lydia smiled. 'Jonno. Daniel and I have been talking, during French. We don't think Mr Scouter should get away with it.'

I was a bit flustered by her bossy glare. 'But what can we do now? We've got nothing. We don't know what went down and we don't know what he's up to. We just have suspicions.' I picked up my knife and fork and tried to carve off a bit of lasagne.

'I know. But he can't get away with all the thieving and the cheating if it was his idea. Justice must be served.' Daniel was now looking very serious.

'He's almost as guilty as her, even if she did the actual murder.' Lydia leaned right in and looked me in the eyes. 'You can't expect us just to walk away now.'

I chewed the tough pasta and had a think. 'I guess we could keep our eyes open, listen in, that sort of thing.'

'We should open a new investigation,' Daniel said decisively. He looked at me, not puppyish this time. 'No one knows he's dirty except us. It's our duty as detectives.'

That made me chuckle a bit, but they didn't join in. They both just sat there, eyes fixed on me, like I had the casting vote and they just needed me to say the word before they leaped into action.

I thought about Kinsey, Jayden, the Boomerangs, the group chat, basketball and all my useless plans to get home and go back to normal.

'We need your help, Jonno. We're a team.'

And then I thought about how the past few days had been some of the most terrifying fun I'd ever had. I *could* be happy here in Hanbridge, with Daniel and Lydia. They were brilliant, strong and fearless. I looked from one to the other.

'OK,' I said. 'Count me in. Let's talk about it in detention.'

Acknowledgements

Thank you to my mum and dad, Margaret and Fred Trethewey, who made sure Cath, Rich, Sarah and I grew up in a house full of music, books and love.

Thanks also to my beloved late grandmother, Mollie Davidson, who always told us funny stories at bedtime.

Thank you to Art Garfunkel and Paul Simon, the soundtrack to my childhood and my bridge over troubled water.

My English teachers, Mrs Christine Jones, Mr David Hasdell, Mrs Peggy West, Mr Mark Ryan and Mrs Carol Groves, made a huge difference to my teenage life. Thank you for extending my frontiers.

I owe a great deal to Dr Cristopher Nash and Vanessa Gajewska for help at critical moments – thank you both.

Sarah Apetrei, Christine Jones, Louisa Franco and Steve Melnikoff read my earliest efforts – heartfelt thanks for your encouragement to keep writing.

Thank you to the Jardines and Jacksons for being wonderfully supportive in-laws.

My friend Helen Luff has had my back since our little ones were little, and always believed in me as an author even though I really didn't. Thank you, lovely Helen.

Thank you, Julia Green and Steve Voake, who admitted me to the wonderful world of the Bath Spa MA in Writing for Young People in 2017; both are exceptional teachers and created a course which nurtured every scrap of ability I possess. I was lucky to be taught by Janine Amos, Jo Nadin, CJ Skuse and Elen Caldecott.

Particular thanks to Elen, who set me on the road to writing this story, and my manuscript tutor Clare Furniss, whose advice and feedback was always spot on.

One of the best things about starting the MA was meeting the Cinnamon Squad – Eve Griffiths, Zulekhá Afzal, Anika Hussain, Fox Terry-Welsh, Kate Den Rooijen and Stephanie Williamson.

These friends held my hand through the bleakest days of the writing, querying and publishing process, and shared in every one of my achievements. 100% would not be here without you; thank you, Squad.

My second-year-MA-friends Lucy Hope, Anna Crowe, Carly Squires and Sarah Stevens – thanks for your feedback and for being such a great example!

My beta-forever Carolyn Ward, whose life has been entangled with my own ever since secondary school – thanks for all the supportive advice and the Twitter links! You are truly inspiring.

Thank you, Maddy and Shaun Sims, for gert lush translation services.

Millie Lean, then a Puffin editor, changed my life in February 2020 when she asked to see more of this manuscript, and gave me constructive feedback and encouragement. I cannot thank you enough, Millie.

A number of Puffin people have since worked on this book, to make it the best that it could be – thank you so much, Katie Sinfield, Wendy Shakespeare, Sarah Connelly, Natalie Doherty, Becky Hydon, Emily Smyth and to Glenn Thomas for illustrating the cover.

Big thanks to my amazing agent Lucy Irvine. You are an incredible advocate and support and I'm so glad you are in my corner.

Graham, Eleanor and Alice, you are my world and I love you millions. Thank you for always being interested, and for supporting me through this whole voyage from occasional scribbler to published author.

Q AND A WITH AUTHOR
LIS JARDINE

How did you come up with the idea of *The Detention Detectives*?

I was studying a course called Writing for Young People, and as part of the course I had to write a novel. Feeling quite stressed at the end of the first term, I re-read *The Clocks* by Agatha Christie to help me relax, and I loved it so much that I decided to write my own murder mystery! I wanted to set it somewhere that any normal kid might find themselves, so I started by listing all the places my daughters went during the week, and one of these was their tennis lessons at the local secondary school. My initial story was called *The Tennis Court Murder*, which later developed into *The Detention Detectives*.

How long did it take you to write?

I started it in 2018 and finished the first draft in six months. I edited it quite a few times and it was accepted by Puffin Books in 2020. I have only just finished the editing process now, so all in all it has taken four years to get as good as it can be!

Were there any challenges in writing the story?

Oh yes! The hardest bit was finding Jonno's voice. I had to write a lot of experimental pieces telling different scenes from his point of view to be sure I knew what made him tick. The actual crime itself was surprisingly easy to come up with (probably because I've read so many murder-mystery novels!)

Which was your favourite part to write?

The ending . . . especially what Jonno and Daniel see out of the window. That made me laugh a lot while I was writing it.

Do you have a favourite character?

Lydia. She's just so epic. I wish I was as sure of myself as she is. I also have a soft spot for Stan Waldron and his pyjamas!

Who designed the cover of the book?

An Australian artist called Glenn Thomas who also does some animation. He has a really cool 90's cartoony style I love.

Who is your favourite detective?

That's so hard. After much thought I'd say it's a three-way tie between Albert Campion (also Jonno's favourite!), Samuel Vimes (the head of the Ankh-Morpork City Watch in Sir Terry Pratchett's superb Discworld novels) and Cadfael (a medieval monk detective in Ellis Peters' historical series). Honourable mention goes to Mrs Bradley, Gladys Mitchell's elderly psychoanalyst detective, who is intimidatingly sharp. That's just the detectives from books – from TV I love *The Mentalist*'s Patrick Jane, Dr. Gregory House, and David Suchet as Poirot!

Were there any particular books that inspired you to write this story?

Novels for young adults were a bit scarce in the UK in the early 1990s, when I was a teenager, so I used to borrow Agatha Christie and Dorothy L. Sayers books from my local library. Ever since,

I have been reading and collecting Golden Age crime novels (crime stories written in the 1920s and 1930s). Being immersed in these tricksy puzzles for so long has influenced my thinking (and plotting!) hugely.

Which books did you enjoy reading as a child?

I read a lot of Enid Blyton. Her books had it all – adventure and investigation and freedom. Her characters got to do so much all by themselves! I also loved the Narnia books, *Anne of Green Gables* (the whole series), Roald Dahl, E. Nesbit and Gene Kemp, and historical novels by Cynthia Harnett.

Which children's books do you wish you could have had on your shelf when you were young?

I didn't know about Diana Wynne Jones's incredible books until I was in my 20s! My childhood self would have absolutely adored them (as I do now). I think I'd also have loved Robin Stevens, Jonathan Stroud, Emma Carroll and Hilary McKay's books too, and Garth Nix's fantasies. I'm also a big fan of Jennifer Killick and Alasdair Chisholm! There are so many brilliant books in bookshops and libraries now, it's hard to know when to stop recommending . . .

If you weren't an author, what job would you like to do?

I would like to test pillows – I am always looking for the right one to get that decent night's sleep! Or I think I'd be a good chocolate/coffee-cake taster. Best of all would be to get paid to read lots of books all day!

Are you working on any new books?

I have a number of projects on the go, most importantly book 2 of *The Detention Detectives* trilogy. This one is told by Lydia, and the crime they're detecting is pretty close to home for her . . .

THE MYSTERY DOESN'T END THERE...

GET READY FOR A
BRAND-NEW
ADVENTURE

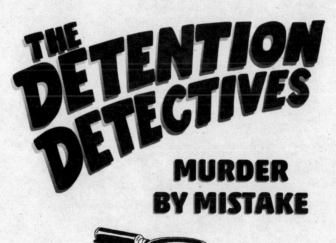

THE DETENTION DETECTIVES

MURDER
BY MISTAKE

COMING JANUARY 2024